T0352987

DAVID GAFFNEY lives in Manchester. He is the author of the novels *Never Never* (2008), *All The Places I've Ever Lived* (2017) and *Out Of The Dark* (2022) plus the flash fiction and short story collections *Sawn-Off Tales* (2006), *Aromabingo* (2007), *The Half-Life of Songs* (2010) and *More Sawn-Off Tales* (2013). His graphic novels with Dan Berry include *The Three Rooms In Valerie's Head* (2018) and *Rivers* (2021).

DAVID GAFFNEY

CONCRETE FIELDS

SALT
MODERN
STORIES

SALT

CROMER

PUBLISHED BY SALT PUBLISHING 2023

2 4 6 8 10 9 7 5 3

First published in Great Britain in 2023 by
Salt Publishing Ltd
12 Norwich Road, Cromer, Norfolk NR27 0AX United Kingdom

www.saltpublishing.com

Salt Publishing Limited Reg. No. 5293401

A CIP catalogue record for this book is available from the British Library

ISBN 978 1 78463 303 5 (Paperback edition)
ISBN 978 1 78463 304 2 (Electronic edition)

Typeset in Granjon by Salt Publishing

Printed and bound in Great Britain by Clays Ltd, Elcograf S.p.A.

For Clare

Contents

CONCRETE FIELDS

The Country Pub

W E NEEDED SOMEWHERE to stay overnight after an event at the Kendal comic book festival and that's when we came across the White Cross Inn. The *Good Food Guide* was gushingly positive on every aspect of this hostelry: its homely, rustic bar, its quaint old bedrooms, and its inspirational, experimental cook, who was pictured in his chef's whites wielding a gleaming, silver knife and smiling through a luxurious beard.

The information was all laid out as if we should have heard of this man, and his dishes were described in detail – things like Orkney mackerel with a rhubarb jus, beetroot bathed in dry ice, and celeriac sorbet, of which there was a photograph, and although you couldn't tell from the picture whether the dessert was made of celeriac or not, it looked well presented, and the venue looked authentically countrified, yet with a shimmer of metropolitan style. So I went online and booked a room for the Saturday night along with a meal in the restaurant.

The event at the comic book festival was to promote my new graphic novel with illustrator Dan Berry, and it went relatively well, apart from a few strange questions from one audience member towards the end which I hadn't quite understood.

On the way to the White Cross Inn, which was somewhere between Kendal and Kirkby Stephen, I raised this with Clare.

'What was that last bloke going on about?' I said.

'Which bloke?'

'The one with the glasses and the Ghoulors sweatshirt.'

'Narrows it down.'

'OK, well, the one who said he couldn't tell if the characters were hugging goodbye or hugging hello in one particular panel?'

'I don't know. It's just good to hear from people who are really engaging in your work, isn't it?'

The White Cross Inn stood next to a ramshackle caravan park, which looked like the sort of caravan park people lived in all the time rather than somewhere you went on your holidays. A board outside the pub advertised soup and a sandwich for £6.50, which struck us as a little unexperimental for our much-lauded chef, but we decided this was probably an ironic touch by this super-arch sophisticate who had probably trained in Copenhagen; the sandwich would be a bowl of liquid and the soup a block of compressed radish gel or something.

Regardless of the food, we both had particular expectations. We had already spoken about the candlelit snug, the log fire, the row of hand-pulled ales on the bar, and the newspapers to read. Possibly there would be a cat to stroke. But when we got inside we were disappointed.

The smaller rooms had been knocked into one large

brightly lit space and all the old-fashioned banquettes from the photos had been ripped out and most of the seating was now in the form of high stools at elevated long tables, like sitting at a breakfast bar in a sitcom. A television on the wall showed a rugby match and it was being watched by two men in orange hi-vis overalls, who were talking in loud voices about someone who had given them some instructions to do some task which had turned out to be in some way impossible.

'If he wants us, he can find us here,' one of them said.

'You can only do what you can do,' the other man said, as I stood next to him at the bar, 'isn't that right, young feller?' he said to me.

'Yep,' I said. 'You can't do more than that.'

We waited for someone to check us in. A squat, solid-looking man with a neck as wide as his shaven head was washing pint glasses behind the bar with his back to us and, although I knew he could see us in the mirror, he didn't make any move to ask us what we wanted.

The only other occupants of the room were a woman and three children. She was sitting at one of the few low tables near the bar with a child on her knee who was playing on an iPad. Two other children were running round the bar, whooping every now and again, but no one seemed to mind. The woman was drinking lager and blackcurrant, not a drink you saw much any more.

I looked at the row of pumps. They didn't have anything that looked remotely like a decent cask ale, only a Bombardier and a Black Sheep; the rest was standard Robinsons, and anyway there wasn't a single corner that looked comfortable enough to sit down and enjoy a good pint in this massive knocked-through space. As well as the noise from the rugby match, the child's game kept making explosive noises and playing tinny tunes.

'Aye,' said the hi-vis man again, to no one in particular. 'You can only do what you can do.'

'As Einstein said,' his friend added.

'Yup.'

A thin woman appeared and looked us up and down, puzzled.

'Ah,' she said. 'You must be from the internet.'

'We've just driven down from Kendal,' I said. 'If that's the same.'

She flipped open a large diary and tapped her finger on an entry. 'You booked online,' she said, as if this was an accusation and it had put her to a lot of trouble.

'And you've got dinner booked as well, haven't you? At eight. I don't think eight is going to be a good idea.' She closed the diary with a snap. 'The local hunt has booked out the rest of the restaurant and they will be ordering their food at eight. So could you come to dinner at seven forty-five instead?'

I looked over into the restaurant, which was large and empty and looked cold and lonely in the way a hotel breakfast room looks when it is all laid for breakfast the next day. 'That's fine,' I said.

'Also,' she said, 'I must warn you that the hunt hasn't actually been out today because the weather wasn't right for the foxes.'

I couldn't help wondering how they could go fox hunting when fox hunting was illegal as far as I knew, but I didn't question this. This was the countryside. You had to respect their ways, I guess.

'So they won't be in a good mood. They'll just want to get really drunk and sing hunting songs,' she said, without smiling.

'I thought fox hunting was illegal?' Clare said.

'Well, it is,' she said, tapping the side of her nose and twisting her mouth up at the side, 'and it isn't.'

She took us through a door behind the bar and up some narrow stairs and then we entered a new extension, in muted greys and cream.

Our room looked like no one had ever stayed in it. There was a small window that you could only see out of if you stood on tip toes and if you did that you saw that it overlooked the caravan park. On the dressing table were two bottles of water and some biscuits wrapped in cellophane. We sat on the bed and looked at each other. The light from the high window was weak and milky. Pale greys and off-whites proliferated, a desaturated palette which looked as though the colours had lost their will to live.

'It must have changed hands,' Clare said.

I picked up a laminated menu the size of a motoring map of Europe. 'Maybe the food will make up for the venue?'

It didn't. There was pie and chips and fish and chips and lasagne and chips. Chilli with half chips and half rice. Each meal was £8.50, which seemed very cheap. Where was the celeriac sorbet and the rhubarb jus? Where was the duck-infused gel? The radish foam?

'Well, it's probably all right. Good old-fashioned pub

grub. But, to be honest, £8.50 a meal? I was hoping to pay more.'

'I know,' she said. 'Me too.'

We didn't eat out a lot, but when we did, we liked it to be worthwhile. So rather then eating out frequently in budget places like Pizza Express, we would save up our money and spend it somewhere a bit posher.

'Well, what should we do while we wait for our dinner? The bar's not very nice to sit in, is it?'

'We could drive into Kirkby Stephen?'

We decided to go for a walk. A footpath from the pub car park led us along the edge of a flat empty field with barbed wire around it. We walked for a quarter of an hour and ended up at the back of the caravan site where there was a hut full of fuel canisters with a bull-terrier tied up outside that barked at us and strained at its leash.

I looked away from the dog to the fields around us. Was this what they called scenery? Was this what they called lovely? Was this what they called natural? It was flat for miles wherever you looked and all you could see were greenish-brown surfaces cropped by sheep, with no distinguishing features to make the landscape interesting.

'There's no trees,' I said.

'I read somewhere that there are more trees in Camden than there are in the Yorkshire Dales or the South Lakes put together. It's the sheep and the farmers. They like to keep it barren like a bowling green. And it also means it floods all the time.'

I looked at the map on my phone. 'There's a village half a mile away. We could walk there? Could be a better pub?'

'Or even a tree.'

But when we got back to the main road and began to walk towards the village, we discovered there were no pavements and cars kept speeding around the bends, often on the wrong side of the road.

'Not only are there no trees,' I said. 'You can't fucking *walk* anywhere to find a tree, you have to drive. Everyone has to drive. I think we should ban the countryside. I don't see the point of it. I don't like the look of it, you can't go anywhere without a car, all people like to do is kill things and eat frozen lasagne and chips and live in shit caravans with barking dogs and drink lager and blackcurrant.'

We decided to brave the bar and have a drink anyway and set off back to the pub.

'What do you think he meant about it, though?'

'Who?'

'The man at the festival with the weird question. About not being able to tell if those characters in that panel were hugging goodbye or hello.'

'Well, I suppose he had a point.'

'Did he?'

'Well, as Dan said in his reply, a still image is a frozen picture. It is a piece of frozen time. It doesn't tell you the immediate past or the immediate future.'

'You were more convinced by Dan's reply than mine, I see.'

Clare stopped walking. 'You know what?' she said. 'Why don't we just go home?'

'What?' I said.

'Well, why spend time somewhere we don't want to be

and eat food we don't want to eat with a bunch of fox
hunters who will be in a bad mood because they haven't
been able to watch their terriers tear a wild animal to pieces,
and then wake up tomorrow somewhere we don't want to
be with nothing to do but drive home?'

'Oh,' I said. 'I hadn't thought of that option.'

'We haven't taken any bags into the room, we haven't
used anything. Did you pay when you booked?'

'No, it was pay when you leave.'

'Let's tell them there's been a family emergency.'

We stood at the bar for about ten minutes until the thin
lady who had checked us in finally came over.

'I'm afraid we've had a call from home to say we have
to go back. There's been a family emergency.'

'Oh,' she said. 'Harold, can you come over here?'

Harold came over. He was the square-shaped man with
the wide neck who had been washing glasses and ignoring
us earlier. He had a goatee beard and tattoos.

'Well, that's a shame,' he said. 'Tell you what, we'll only
charge you for the room, as you never actually ordered any
food. But we'll have to charge you for breakfast because
we got a few things in.'

Everything suddenly felt very odd to me, as if the landlord and landlady knew that all of this was going to happen
and had prepared for it. It was as if the whole scene had
happened before and was repeating itself. And I was the
only one who didn't know the script.

'Oh, I don't know,' I said. 'We haven't even unpacked.
We haven't been in the room for more than five minutes. I
didn't think we would need to pay anything. After all, it's
a family emergency?'

I decided not to mention the fact that the pub was nothing like the one advertised on the internet with its celeriac sorbet and fancy chef, because the landlord would no doubt say, well look, we do food, we do beer, we have a bar, we have bedrooms, what's your problem? He would probably argue that his food was better value than a dollop of rhubarb jus and a sliver of venison for thirty quid. He would claim they had improved the place, not ruined it. And if you asked the locals – the blokes who had been watching the rugby, the woman with the three kids – they would agree with him. Who wanted to drink in a dark, dingy pub with beer that smelt of wet dogs, that was heated by an ineffective open fire, that had no TV? And who wanted to spend a week's wages on a minuscule portion of some gimmicky dish that probably didn't even come on a normal plate? Maybe I was in the wrong. What sort of middle-class monster had I become?

'Well, I'm afraid you've booked,' he said. 'So you have to pay. That's how hotels work. We have lost out. We could have booked that room out to someone else.'

I looked over at the board on which the room keys hung and saw that only one was missing – ours – but I didn't say anything.

'I'm sorry,' I said. 'If you want to, you can send me the bill. I'll give you my address.'

'I suppose that's what we will have to do,' he said, and slammed down the pad of bills and picked up another pad of paper.

I told him our address and when I said Manchester, the landlady (his wife, I assumed) shook her head as if to say, typical, it's what you would expect. As he wrote, the landlord's brow became red and sticky with sweat. I looked at his hand holding the pen; his knuckles were white and his hand was shaking. All my years spent working as a welfare benefits adviser had taught me how to recognise rage building up, and this man was about to blow.

As we left the pub I heard the landlord lift up the side of the bar as if he was about to follow us and we crossed the car park briskly as I imagined the landlord's eyes burning into my back with hatred. Even the car we were in made us look bad. It was hired. I hadn't owned a car for years, but the landlord and landlady of the White Cross Inn weren't to know that, and although I always booked the cheapest model, the hire company had run out of budget hatchbacks, and I had been upgraded to a BMW 3 Series. Running away without paying a bill of fifty quid in a sixty-grand glossy black saloon.

'I just need to get something out of the boot,' said Clare as we reached the vehicle.

I jumped in the driver's seat and threw open the passenger door. 'No! We just need to get away. That man looked seriously angry.'

I reversed out of the parking space without looking round, and we spun out of the car park into the road, gravel flying out behind, and as I sped away the car's engine began to moan at a higher and higher pitch and I realised I was doing sixty in third gear and so I quickly changed up to fourth, then fifth, and for a split second I was in such a state of heightened stress that I wasn't sure whether we were speeding away from the pub or back to it. 'Is this the right way?' I shouted to Clare. 'We are not heading back there, are we?'

'Yes, it's the right way,' she said. 'Just drive.'

Three or four miles down the road, I slowed down.

'Do you think he'll follow us?' said Clare.

'No. He'll have to just write it off as a bad debt. Those people were fraudulent, leaving all that stuff on the internet about the old menu and the old chef and the old bar.'

'But that's not what you said, is it?'

'No.'

'I'm worried. Should we have paid?'

'Morally, no. I think they're taking the piss. But technically and legally, yes, we should have paid. You are supposed to pay for a hotel if you book it.'

'He's got our address. What if he turns up at the door?'

'He's not going to come all the way to Manchester and spend money on petrol and parking.'

'He won't have to park. He can just stop his car outside our house. You are obsessed with paying for parking. It's something I've never liked about you.'

'Anyway, he's not going to put himself even further out of pocket coming to Manchester when he knows we won't answer the door.'

'Maybe he'll send someone. The boys. They talk about sending the boys round, don't they? This is the hospitality business. They're all gangsters. Maybe he'll look us up on social media and put things online.'

'He didn't look like a social media kind of person.'

'She will be, though.'

It started to rain and the windscreen wipers came on automatically and began slapping to and fro really fast and I couldn't work out how to turn them off. A red light appeared on the dashboard and a message flashed up saying that we should stop immediately.

'These modern cars have artificial intelligence,' said Clare. 'It knows we've done something wrong and it is suggesting we go back and put things right.'

'Do you think BMW programme a moral code into their cars?'

'Probably not. But I bet Citroën do.'

The car began to go slower and slower, the engine sounding like a Hoover powering down. Then it turned itself off completely and we glided along until I found a narrow road to turn off into, and I rolled the car up it and on to a bank of grass. We sat there for a few moments not saying anything. Rain pelted down and neither of us wanted to get out. My phone had no signal.

'There's some lights over there,' I said. 'It looks like a village. Let's see if there's a pub we can wait in while I ring the car hire company.'

There was a pub – the Golden Hind – and when we stepped inside it was like walking into heaven. A log fire was burning in the grate, there were a few couples dotted about drinking and reading newspapers, and several tables were laid out for dinner. A row of hand pumps on the bar had handwritten labels on them and there was a detailed blackboard telling you all about the beer.

Violins played and angelic voices sang.

'What an intelligent car,' I said, and, to the landlord, 'You don't by any chance have rooms as well, do you?'

'We do,' he said. 'And the room is half price if you have a meal here with us.' He handed me a piece of paper with curly handwriting on it. 'It's a small, carefully curated menu.

Just what's fresh on the day and whatever we can forage locally. The wines are all paired with the food. There's a table free at eight, if you'd like it?'

Later we were sitting by the fire sipping a real ale from the local micro-brewery. We were the only ones left in the pub by then, and we had already been shown our room, which was a tiny, dusty space in a slopey-ceilinged attic that smelt of damp. A creaky brass four-poster was covered by a candlewick bedspread. But despite it looking like your granny's house, it had a charm and character that the other place could never achieve with its Instagrammable mini-malism. The whole pub was crooked as if it had subsided, and going down the dark, wonky stairs to the bar made you feel as if you were descending through a German expressionist film set.

There were plenty of logs on the fire, so we had a few more drinks and did the *Guardian* crossword together.

At about midnight the landlord came over. 'I'm off now,' he said. 'All the staff are gone.'

'Do we have to go up to our room?'

'No, it's fine,' he said. 'You can sit here by the fire as long as you like. Throw as many logs on as you want and don't worry about putting it out when you leave. It will take care of itself.' He spoke very slowly and looked to the side all the time, rather than straight at us. 'I live a few miles away, in the town, in Kirkby Stephen. We lived here above the pub for a while but, you know, it was quite lonely for my wife. She didn't like the dark and the—' He raised his hand and rubbed his fingers together in the air as if trying to catch something invisible '—the mystery. The mystery of living in the countryside. She's very practical. She thinks you have to be superstitious to enjoy the countryside. She thinks people who like the countryside tend to believe in things that aren't really there.' He paused and looked down at his shoes. 'She was brought up in the suburb of a big city. So there's just my brother upstairs. But he won't bother you. You won't see him or hear him at all.' He looked up at the ceiling, and then down again. 'He's been sick, you see, quite ill for the last few years, and he doesn't really like people that much.' The landlord took out his car keys. 'Anyway, if you want anything from the bar, just help yourselves, write down on that pad what you've had, and we'll settle up tomorrow.'

When he had gone, we heard a heavy door slamming followed by the jangling of keys and a clunking noise as the lock was engaged. A car engine started and ran for a few minutes before we heard the wheels crunching on gravel as the vehicle left the car park. And then all was silent.

'People in the countryside are so trusting,' I said. 'Imagine a bar in Manchester leaving you alone and telling you to drink whatever you want. Look at all those single malt whiskies.'

'We shouldn't betray his trust.'

'We'll pay for it, of course,' I said.

'Let's just have another beer. I'm getting quite tired.'

I placed another log on the fire and we sat in silence gazing at the embers and sipping our ale.

'Going back to what Dan said about that panel,' Clare said. 'About still images being like pieces of frozen time? Think about a photograph of a man holding a hat above his head. You don't know whether he is putting the hat on or taking it off, do you?'

'In the case of our graphic novel,' I said, 'shouldn't you know from the expression Dan draws on the characters' faces?'

'Or maybe from the words you've supplied?'

'Yes. But just relying on the words to say everything is a bit of a cop-out. A graphic novel should be first and foremost a visual medium.'

There was a loud thump from above our heads. We looked at the ceiling. A door catch went click then there was another thump and then a low moaning sound like someone had left the room but suddenly realised they had forgotten something important. A door clicked again followed by steps on the stairs. Then the footsteps stopped and there was no more sound.

'I wonder where he's going?'

'I don't know,' I said.

We listened hard but couldn't hear anything any more.

'I wonder what being sick meant.'

'I'm sure it will be fine.'

I poured us each a whisky as a nightcap and we drank it in silence looking at the fire. Orange and yellow sparks shot out. Everything became amplified as if my senses had been heightened: the sour notes of the whisky, the intense odour of burning logs, the spitting, hissing fire, the whiff of disinfectant from the toilets. Then from the stairs came a repetitive, rasping noise, like rapid, heavy breathing or someone sawing wood. We looked at each other. Clare gripped my hand. The sawing sound began again and went on for what seemed like ages, then stopped.

There was a long silence.

With a bang, the door behind the bar flew open and a

man staggered backwards into the room, looking as though he was dragging something large and awkward. He turned his head and spotted us, dropped whatever he had been dragging, and began to move slowly in our direction. A couple of feet away from us he stopped and something like a small smile appeared on his face. Then everything became blurry, and for a moment I didn't know whether the man was coming towards us or moving away and it's still like that.

The Garages

I BOUGHT THE house in Macclesfield that Ian Curtis used to live in and I had only been moved in a day and a half when the neighbour who lived opposite came over and asked me if John Ireland had been round.

'I don't know,' I said. 'What does he look like?'

'Big feller with crooked teeth,' the man said.

'No. No one's been round yet. You're the first.' I said.

'He'll come round, John Ireland, and he'll ask you if he can buy the lease on your garage,' the man said.

'What should I say?'

'Well, it depends on whether you want to sell the lease on your garage or not.'

There was a set of eight garages at the top of the road, their doors painted with lustrous black gloss, and they presented an intimidating blank wall of wood you had to walk past every day. I wondered what Ian Curtis had thought of this black wall.

'Who is John Ireland and why does he want my garage?'

'He's bought the other seven garages and we think – the street – that he wants them all.'

I thought it odd that the street had thoughts – or rather

that this man imagined that the street had thoughts – and I wondered how he tuned into them.

'Oh, OK,' I said.

'Yours will complete the set.'

'Did the previous owner not want to sell it?'

'No. The previous owner of your place had a classic car. It's only people with classic cars who need garages, nowadays. It's the insurance.'

'What was the car?'

'1960s Sunbeam.'

'Nice.'

'Yes. But you don't have a classic car, do you?'

'No.'

'Well then, he'll definitely expect you to sell it to him.'

I wondered how I might use the garage if I kept it. I could store things in it. But my possessions consisted mainly of records and books, items which would not fare well in an old damp garage. I really couldn't think of any use for it and if the price was right I must admit I would be happy to sell it to anyone. I didn't even mind what he wanted to use it for.

'Is it connected to Ian Curtis?'

'No. Definitely not. John Ireland doesn't know anything about Joy Division. And Ian Curtis never owned that garage anyway. It was bought by a later owner, off someone else.'

'These garages always seem to be changing hands then.'

The man paused to watch a silver Ford Focus crawl up the street and turn to go past the black garages before it disappeared from view.

'Yes. It looks that way.'

◊

The following evening John Ireland knocked on the door. He was a tall man, and wide, like a rugby player, with ruddy skin that looked soft, and I noticed the crooked teeth the neighbour had told me about, which I was surprised at because he looked from his clothes to be the sort of person who could afford to get those sorted out.

'I wondered if you wanted to sell the lease on your garage,' he said.

'I'm not sure,' I said.

'Well if you're not sure,' he said, 'have a think about it. I'll pop round next week.'

'How much are you offering?'

'Well the going rate is £2,500. So how about that, plus £250 as a sweetener?'

'Right,' I said.

There seemed no harm in it and the money was attractive. But I decided I would take the option of the week he had offered me to think about it.

The next day I explored the area a bit more. I walked past the row of black garages and stopped at the end of the street, where it met the main road, which was a steep hill that continued in a straight line all the way down into the centre of Macclesfield. I looked down the hill and thought about how strange it was that this part of the town was so high up. I'd been used to living in south Manchester where everywhere was flat. I crossed the road and went into the park where there was a group of middle-aged women playing crown green bowls. I watched them for a time.

Then I went over to a run-down-looking leisure centre with metal shutters over the window. A gaudy mural had been painted on its walls, depicting smoking mill chimneys and industrial scenes, a bit like a 1970s hippy version of a Lowry painting. Behind me, a woman on a small electric mobility scooter went past with a large grass-cutting vehicle driving close behind her, trying to overtake. She pulled in to the side and let the large vehicle pass, waving at its driver as he accelerated away. Then when he had gone she continued towards the main road, heading, I assumed, for the shops.

I went back to the row of black garages. They looked abandoned, as if no one had ever opened them in their whole existence. I wondered why they were all painted black, and not different colours to reflect the personalities of the different people who owned them. Then I remembered that they were all owned by John Ireland. Apart from mine.

The following week John Ireland knocked on the door and when I answered he asked me if I had made up my mind.

'What about?' I said.

'Selling the garage.'

'Oh. Yes,' I said. 'You can have the garage.'

'Great,' he said. 'Do you want to go through a solicitor?'

'I don't know,' I said.

'How about a gentlemen's agreement?'

'That would be fine,' I said.

John Ireland came into the hall and sat down on the stool that I kept there for these sorts of occasions. He brought out a chequebook and a small stubby ballpoint pen from his inside pocket and wrote me a cheque for the amount we had agreed and held it out to me. But before I took it I said, 'There's one condition.'

'What's that?' he asked, yanking his hand away from me as if I was about to set his cheque on fire.

'I'd like to know why you want to own all the garages and what you keep in them.'

'Then the deal is off,' he said, and he lifted the cheque up in front of my face and tore it in two, with an expression on his face of intense concentration, as if he was listening very carefully to the tearing sound it made. He stood up, stuffed the two halves into his back pocket, walked quickly towards the door, and put his hand on the handle. Then he turned round to face me, as if to say something, but must have thought better of it, because he turned away again, threw open the door, and left. I went to the doorway and watched him stomp down the road and round the corner. I knew he would enter the Frog and Railway and sit on his own at the end of the bar, scowling into his beer, because I had often seen him through the window in the same position when I passed the pub on my way to the bus stop.

Another week passed and every evening of that week, at different times, I saw John Ireland standing outside my garage, staring at it. When I went over to say hello he didn't answer, just shook his head and moved away down the road as if he'd been doing something entirely normal.

Eventually I cracked and went to find him in the Frog and Railway. He was sitting on his favourite high stool at the end of the bar, watching, or pretending to watch, a European football match on the large screen. I sat down next to him and looked ahead at the mirror and all the whiskies, gins, brandies, and liqueurs.

'Listen,' I said. 'I don't really care why you want to own all the garages. If it means that much to you, you can have it. You can drop off the cheque tomorrow. Here's the key.'

He turned slowly to face me and I don't think I have ever seen a man look so happy. He took the key and gripped it tightly in his fist for a few moments. Then he shuddered and closed his eyes before letting out a small, barely audible whimper. It was as though some uncanny power was being transferred to him from that small metal object. When he opened his eyes again they were full of tears and he squeezed my shoulder, and looked me straight in the face.

'Thank you so much,' he said. 'This is not something that a man like you could ever understand.'

As I watched him leave I looked at his half-finished pint on the bar and wondered what he meant by *a man like me*. I didn't know I was *a man like me*. I never knew what people meant when they talked about me like that, saying things like *I think you're really going to like this* or *I don't think this will be your type of thing* or *you're not really the sort of person we are aiming this at.*

Later that night I was eating a kebab from the Ghost Chilli takeaway in town while watching out of my window and I saw John Ireland walk up the street and over to his now wholly owned row of black garages. He opened up his new acquisition with the key I had given him and I was glad to see that it worked because I hadn't even opened it myself to see what was in there. It was an up-and-over door and he reached in and flipped a switch and when light flooded the space I could see even from that distance that the garage was completely empty. He didn't go inside, just looked at this empty space for a long time and then closed the door again, locked the padlock, and after a long pause, patted the door of the garage as if it were the flank of a much-loved animal. There was a noticeable spring in his step when he set off back down the road to his little terraced house.

The next time I saw him he was with his wife and two kids in the supermarket and it surprised me to see he had a partner and family as I had associated his multiple garage-buying habit and his lone drinking with the life of a single man. When he was with his family he seemed much more cheery and he waved over at me and called out my name.

'Hi,' I said. 'Are you enjoying the garage?'

'Very much so,' he said. 'Thanks a lot. You don't know how much it means to me.'

His wife was standing slightly behind him. She was a tall thin woman with a pale happy-looking face, and a dark black bob of hair. She was smiling and looked like one of those people who always smiled even when they were telling you something serious.

She rolled her eyes at me and her smile grew even broader.

'I have no idea what goes on in his head,' she said. Then she put her hand on his shoulder. 'But if it makes him happy, what's the problem? How are you enjoying the street? What with the children and work we never get a chance to see the neighbours at all.' I went to answer her but John Ireland seemed to give her some sort of imperceptible signal that she must end the conversation.

'Ah, so sorry,' she said, 'we have to drop the kids off at a party – catch you soon,' and they turned and moved down the aisle – at a very slow pace, I thought, for people who claimed to be in a hurry.

After the sale I watched the garages carefully from my window, and I never saw John Ireland attend to them at any time. I was at home a lot and had plenty of opportunities to make these observations, which were very thorough and covered several different times of day including the middle of the night. John Ireland never visited any of the garages to open them, to put anything in, or take anything away, or to check that whatever was held inside them was safe. Nor did he appear to have sub-let them to anyone else.

I kept meaning to get him into conversation and see if I could find out what was in them, but apart from the time with his family in the supermarket, he always avoided me. If I saw him in the park, watching the middle-aged women playing crown green bowls, he would move off when he saw me coming. If he was in the Frog and Railway he would leave as soon as I entered.

A year later his wife called round and asked me if she could come inside.

I let her in and she stood in the same place John Ireland had stood when he first asked about the garage. Her usually neat black bobbed hair looked ragged and in need of a trim, her pale face was greyer, and her smile, though it was there, made fewer creases at the edges of her eyes.

She asked me if I wanted the garage back.

'Doesn't John need it any more?' I said.

'Oh, didn't you know?' she said. 'John died.'

'Oh,' I said. 'I'm so sorry, I had no idea. What happened?'

She told me that John Ireland had been killed on a building site where he was working as a quantity surveyor. A crane had been lifting a heavy digger and it had swung out unexpectedly and crushed him against a wall. She and the children were devastated. 'John and I met at technical college when we were teenagers and neither of us has ever dated anyone else.'

Her smile disappeared for a few moments and she stared at me with an intense expression as if she were looking at an upside-down map of something she knew well and trying to make sense of it.

I didn't know what to say. I told her I wasn't bothered about the garage.

'But,' I said, 'I did always wonder what he wanted them all for?'

'It's odd,' she said. 'Can I sit down?'

I took her into the kitchen, and she sat at the table and looked out of the window at the row of black garage doors as she spoke.

'John had this very particular view about the world. He thought that life was too busy and that every space was always too full of objects and clutter and possessions. Not long after we'd met he told me that one day he'd like to own a space with absolutely nothing in it. Once he owned a space with nothing in it he would be happy. So when we moved here he bought one of the garages and kept it completely empty. And it made him happy. But then he wanted more, and that's when he started buying up the rest of the row. The more empty garages he owned, the happier he was. He said that it relaxed him. At night, if he couldn't sleep, all he had to do was think of that row of empty garages and he would drift off like a baby. After he'd bought the last garage in that row, your garage, he even started thinking about buying garages in other streets and even other towns, and keeping them all empty. "Imagine that," he used to say, "Imagine garages all over the country, even all over the world, all with nothing in them but empty space. What a wonderful thing that would be." Oh, I miss him so much,' she said, finally, and then she started to cry and I put my hand on her arm, lightly, and I looked out at the garages just as she was.

When she had gone I went upstairs and lay on the bed. I thought about the empty garage. I thought about the walls, the plain bare walls. I thought about the inside of the door, blank from edge to edge in all four directions. I thought about the dark corners with nothing in them but balls of dust and I thought about the bare ceiling and the bare floor. I thought of the mounds of unshelved books and records that filled every space in my own house and I vowed that the next day I would do something important to commemorate the life of John Ireland. I just didn't know what it would be.

The Staring Man

A PLASTIC SILVER birch from the edge of the paddling pool had been snapped off during transportation and Charlotte was gluing it back on when the old man came over. He had delicate, almost transparent skin, and his pale blue watery eyes were so deep set they looked as if they were sinking into his face.

'I thought that this might help with the consultation,' he said, handing her a sheet of A4 paper.

It was a black and white photograph of a young couple dangling a baby's feet in the water of the original paddling pool.

He prodded the image. 'That's me. That's my wife Dorothy, and that's Heather. She's three there. 1958.'

The couple looked innocently happy, their small trim frames somehow weightless, as if in those days there had been less gravity.

'You can keep it. I have the original.'

'Thanks very much,' said Charlotte. 'We could display it next to the model. If that would be OK?'

'Please do,' he said, and then began to walk around Charlotte's scale model of the refurbished park and its amenities, looking at it from every possible angle, as curious as if it were a 3D map of his own mind.

'I didn't know there were people like you,' he said after a time.

'There's a need for it,' Charlotte said. 'We make things smaller so that people can understand them better.'

'So then what happens? You show it to the families and the old men who sit in the sun, and see if they like it?'

'Yes,' she said.

'And if they don't?'

'They can go and fuck themselves,' Charlotte said.

The old man looked at her for a while, then laughed.

'Your role is not usually outward-facing?'

'You got it,' she said.

'How do you know where to place each human figure? Do you have,' he paused and looked to the side, '"artistic freedom"?'

'At an away day in a spa hotel they filled a flip chart. The models should not look like separate individuals, but like a group who are co-operating. They should look intelligent and altruistic.'

The old man tickled the head of one of the model people as if it were a small animal. 'They do indeed look like that,' he said.

'Oh, and they read periodicals.'

'I have no idea how you achieve it, Miss –?'

'Charlotte, call me Charlotte.' She put out her hand and the old man shook it. He was wearing a trilby hat with a fishing feather in it like her grandfather used to.

'I have to convey all that from their position in the model and how they are spaced in relation to each other.'

'And they all look exactly the same,' the old man said.

'Yes,' said Charlotte. 'It's kind of a serving suggestion.'

'I'm called Jones, by the way. Ted Jones.'

His eyes were dragged towards a certain figure at the edge of the paddling pool, and he bent down and looked at it intently.

'Why is that man staring up at the sky?' he said. 'It looks as if he has spotted a plane about to crash, or a storm coming in. Sorry, I was an English teacher and my imagination runs away.'

The miniature person he was referring to was one of Charlotte's favourites and, like the three-legged dog in a Ken Loach film, he appeared in every model she made.

'Staring man,' Charlotte said. 'He adds something intangible. Takes you out of the model and makes you feel there is something beyond. In my last project I stood him beside an abattoir and people said he added a spiritual dimension, as if he was searching for God in a world where people killed things.'

Ted Jones went quiet when she said this, and glanced towards the door. Then his pale eyes flicked all over the model again, searching.

'What I find strange,' he said, 'is that I see no staff.'

She pointed to a low building of liver-coloured bricks. 'That's the park keeper's office.'

'Is he there now?' said Ted Jones.

'Ah, Mr Jones,' she said. 'No. We don't model the things you can't see.'

The old man didn't seem to have anything else to say and for a spell they stared at the stilled little figures on the scale model. The sounds of children's voices drifted in from the school nearby.

'Do you have any older photographs?' Charlotte said, eventually.

'No,' he said. 'The past. You move on, don't you? Concrete over it.'

'I thought maybe your parents might have used the pool.'

He took off his trilby and sat down at the side of the model.

'My parents were Catholic and devoutly religious, and when they found out Dorothy had been divorced they told me that they were not so bothered about seeing me any more. I tried everything, but they tore up my letters and posted back the shreds.'

Charlotte sat down next to him 'But what about—'

'Heather. Yes. When we had Heather, little Heather, I thought that would change their minds. But the minute they clapped eyes on that child, my parents grimaced and turned away. "God did this thing to you for a reason," my mother said. "God sent you that poor girl because of your sins. That's what happens when you turn your back on your faith." I never saw them again. Didn't want to, after that. Family bonds, they say you can't break them. But you can, and sometimes they can never be fixed. Me and Dorothy were not in the least upset by Heather's condition. We loved her, loved her more than any person can love another person, and she loved us back.'

'You must bring them both here, to see my scale model,' said Charlotte.

'They passed away. Dorothy was 87 and Heather, well. She had only a certain time allotted. In some ways it's for the best. Who would have looked after Heather when we were gone?'

Ted Jones picked up his trilby, put it on his head, and smiled at her, his pale eyes searching her face as if she might have an answer to his problems from the past.

'That's so sad, Mr Jones,' she said. 'Come back and look at my model any time you like.'

After Ted Jones left, Bill Godfrey came over. He was from the Friends of Chorlton Park and had a stud earring, friendship bracelets, and was wearing a short-sleeved shirt bestrewn with stars. Charlotte stiffened, readying herself for more abuse about the low-quality specifications for the new paddling pool.

'Is that Ted Jones?' he said, nodding at the photograph.

'Yes,' she said.

'You can't use that picture.'

'It's simply a matter of asking Mr Jones to sign some forms.'

'Do you know the circumstances?'

'I have to get back to my office now.'

'They loved that girl. Couldn't bear to think of what would happen to her after they died. He and Dorothy were in their mid-eighties, Heather over fifty. She never went out on her own and Ted and Dorothy couldn't bear to imagine her in a care home. Ted couldn't get the problem out of his mind, he went over and over it. He spoke to Social Services, everyone, but no solution satisfied him.'

'It's a photograph of a happy family,' Charlotte said. 'It will add a nice human dimension.'

'Then, one Sunday teatime,' Bill Godfrey continued, 'Dorothy and Heather were sitting holding hands on the sofa like they always did, watching their favourite TV programme, *Antiques Roadshow*, and Ted saw them lounging there as happy as anything and, in his words, he felt an enormous rush of love like a tidal surge. He went out to the shed, found a claw hammer and took it back into the house with him. He phoned the police immediately afterwards and told them what he had done. You wouldn't guess it, would you? A retired headteacher, respectable, peace-loving.'

Charlotte sat down. She took off her glasses and placed them on the table. She pulled her long hair back into a ponytail and secured it with a rubber band.

Bill Godfrey watched her in silence. 'Not all old people are nice,' he said finally. 'I'm sorry,' and he stalked off into the kitchen where she heard him clattering about with cups and saucers, preparing the tea and sandwiches for the evening consultees.

Outside, the bushes were thickening with indigo shadows. She looked at the staring man in the model, then through the window at the sky, and thought about how poorly her model reflected the real world, with its smells, its sounds, its shapes and shades. She pulled the staring man away from his fixings, prised the park keeper's building up from its base, and put him inside it, lying on his back and looking up at the ceiling. No one would ask what his function was any more. Her model would be just a model, and nothing else.

The Painting

ONE THURSDAY AFTERNOON a few years ago I was driving along when I had a strong sense that I was being followed. It was a hot summer's day and I was heading to a secret pool that only a few people know about on a section of the river Esk in west Cumbria, with the ridiculous aim of teaching myself to swim, and I became certain that the vehicle behind was tailing me. The car was a red Citroën 2CV and had been stuck to me like a shadow all the way from Whitehaven. I decided that the test would be when I turned off the A595 towards Wasdale and sure enough, the 2CV followed. It kept itself a little way back from me so I couldn't see the driver, but it stayed there all the way down this twisting road. It took the next turn I took as well, down an even more obscure road which was a single track with passing places. I slowed down and allowed him to creep up closer and saw that it was driven by a man with a long beard wearing a straw hat. Maybe he realised he was intruding by getting so close, so he slowed down and as the road was full of twists and turns, I lost sight of him for a mile or so. At the next passing place I pulled in and turned off the engine and waited for a few minutes. Sure enough the 2CV with the hat and the long beard inside sailed past. So I set off again, this time driving quite close to him, and eventually he pulled in at a passing place and waved me past.

The next few miles were passed without further sightings of him, so I turned off again, on to the unsignposted farmer's track I knew about, and at the end of it, parked next to a gate that said Beware of the Bull. I got out of the car, crossed an empty field, and at the other end located the almost hidden path overgrown with brambles. This path always felt longer than I remembered, as if it was leading nowhere. But after a time I emerged into a wooded area and could hear the rushing of water. On the other side of the trees was a clearing where there was a curve in the river and fallen branches and rocks had slowed the water's passage to form a deep still pool.

I sat down on the bank and looked at the river for a short time. In this hot weather the pool looked inviting even to a non-swimmer like me. My friends and I used to come here all the time when we were teenagers. The pool was so deep you could climb the overhanging trees and jump in, which my friends did over and over while I, the anxious non-swimmer, watched from my place on the bank.

I looked behind me to see if the man with the beard in the red 2CV car had followed. But of course not. Why would I be followed? I was not a spy or a criminal.

Until now, being unable to swim had not seemed like a big deal. However, there was a girl I was interested in who liked to talk about swimming in wild places like quarries and tarns. She felt so free, so close to nature, when she was in wild water. It was elemental, like being reborn. The air became her flesh and the water became her bones, her body an unending wave. I wanted to feel like that. I was generally a worried, awkward person and maybe swimming in some isolated muddy pond would loosen me up. An ice-cold hit of wild water could restart your system, like turning yourself on and off again, and that's something I felt I could really do with.

I undressed down to my swimming shorts and, keeping my trainers on in case of rusted farm tools or dead sheep, waded into the pool. The cold water crept up my body but I kept going deeper, making pathetic *ah ah* sounds until I was up to my chin. Then I stopped and stood still for a time. It was so quiet. All around me the trunks of trees and fallen logs were lagged with moss and ferns and they seemed to insulate the place against any sound from the outside world. Small birds cheeped, a raven coughed and, high above, I heard the shriek of a buzzard riding on a thermal. With its pin-sharp vision this raptor would be able to see the top of my head, and I wondered whether he might mistake it for easy prey and dive down to try and carry me off.

I had heard that the best way to gain confidence in water is to float on your back, and as I was afraid of putting my face in the river more than anything, that seemed like a good place to start. So I plucked up courage, stretched my arms out to the side and closed my eyes. It would be like falling backwards on to a feather mattress on which I would be able to float for hours. I drew in a long breath, lifted my feet off the river bed and tipped my head back, and to my astonishment I didn't end up on the bottom eating grit. It worked. I was floating. I opened my eyes and stared up at the blue sky enjoying the sensation of the cold water lapping at the back of my head. For a few moments I luxuriated in this unique feeling of weightlessness. There was not a single cloud in the sky, and long vapour trails led my eye to a jet plane moving north towards Scotland where, at Lockerbie, it would veer off over the Atlantic towards the USA. I wondered whether I could paint this scene, but rather than depict it figuratively, I would turn it into one of my abstract canvasses, capture the mood rather than the colours and shapes. I felt I was good at that, and although most people who looked at my paintings saw only a turbulent squall of lumpy paint, trowelled and spooned onto the surface, I felt that these canvases really said something. If you looked properly you would see that they spoke about an experience, an emotion. Rather than replicating the world as it is, they held within them the force of their production, the sweeps and the flicks, the smudging and the scraping, waiting to be released.

I floated like that, thinking about my next painting, for what I thought was ages but must have been only a couple of minutes until I heard the snap of a branch and I abruptly righted myself, making a lot of splashing noise in the water.

I stood there with the water up to my chin, looking over to the bank.

The 2CV man with his beard and straw hat emerged from the woods, sat down on the bank and stared at the water. Either he hadn't noticed me or he was pretending not to know I was there. I considered my situation. He didn't look dangerous in his clownish headgear, ZZ Top beard and Dr Martens shoes; yet I didn't feel entirely safe standing there nearly naked, up to my chin in cold water, with my clothes, shoes, phone, wallet, and the keys to my mother's car on the river bank.

The buzzard shrieked, a chainsaw moaned in the distance, and, from further away, an axe went thud thud thud, echoing back a split second later from the other side of the valley.

The man leaned back against a tree trunk and stretched his legs out in front of him. He continued to stare into the water and still did not register my presence. Perhaps the shade from the trees had created distracting shadows and patterns.

Then he took out a hand-rolled cigarette, lit it with a Zippo, and blew out smoke. The smell of weed wafted over. We both looked at the water. Shafts of sunlight had turned clouds of tiny flies into dancing silver specks.

'I never knew about this hidden place,' he said.

'You been here before?'

'No. I followed you.'

He tilted up his head towards me and smiled awkwardly as if to say *there you are I've admitted it, you caught me!*

'Oh right,' I said, trying to sound casual, but aware that my voice had begun to sound high and constricted. 'I've done that before myself – you see a car turn off down a road you've never noticed before and you think oh I'd like to see what's down there.'

'We all like to know what other people are doing, don't we?'

He looked down river, to the point where it curled round the bend and disappeared into a dark copse of trees.

'Fresh air and countryside. We are supposed to like it because it's natural. But this?' he waved his arm at the scenery around us. 'This is just an outdoor factory for wood and wool, don't you think?'

'I don't know.'

'There used to be pelicans and white-tailed eagles. Bears and wolves. Animals that kept you on your toes. Natural. Why is being natural a good thing, anyway? Nothing we do as humans is natural. We feel sad when nothing has made us sad, we feel afraid when there is nothing to be frightened of. That's not natural, is it?'

'I take it you're not a fan of the great outdoors.'

'Not an official card-carrying member of the club, no.'

'So what brings you here this evening, to the middle of nowhere?'

'I just wanted to have a little chat with you about something.'

'Do I know you?'

'No – but I know you. Mr floating head on the river.'

The water around me had begun to feel colder and I was aware I was shivering. I couldn't have put myself in a more vulnerable situation. I imagined leaping up Tarzan-like, grabbing an overhanging branch and delivering a flying kick to his head – but this was the stuff of comic books.

'I don't know if I'll be any help to you with anything. This is all a bit weird, to be honest. Could you just send me an email?'

'Yes, sorry, but this needs to be face to face. I'm Jane Patterson's husband – Mrs Patterson, your old art teacher.'

Now I was even more confused. I left sixth form last year, and while it was true Mrs Patterson had been my A-Level art tutor, I hadn't had much to do with her personally. She had made a strong impression on the class, it was true – she was one of those younger teachers that the boys all had crush on and, being only a few years or so older than us sixth formers, she had seemed even attainable to some. But although I had enjoyed my art classes with Mrs Patterson, my abstract canvasses laden with thick colour failed to impress the exam board, earning me an ungraded mark.

'She was a great teacher,' I said.

'She's been unwell for a while.'

'Sorry to hear that.'

'I think you can help us.'

'I've no idea how,' I said. 'But can we discuss it somewhere a little more normal? Maybe when one if us is not half-submerged in a river.'

He took out a scrap of paper and wrote something on it and then dropped it on my pile of clothes. Then he took off his straw hat, and made a strange awkward bow.

'So sorry to disturb your private bathing.'

And with that he disappeared into the woods.

Back in Whitehaven, I parked my car on the street and took one of the narrow side passages down towards the market place. On the way I passed the 2CV parked on the main street on an hour's parking limit and noticed the parking display card showing that he had arrived fifteen minutes ago. I found a position near the market place and spotted Mr Patterson sitting on the bandstand scanning the crowds.

I retraced my steps to my car and drove out of the town and up to the Loop Road where he and his wife lived. It had been easy to locate them in a town as small as this.

When Jane Patterson opened the door she looked like

a woman in a trance. Her eyes roved over my face, then down my clothes, then to my shoes, then back, and then sideways past me into the street.

'It's David, isn't it?' she said after a time. 'You made the painting.'

'The painting?'

'Yes. My husband has been looking for you. We've been trying our best to solve it on our own but it's been a long time and now we are desperate. Finding you and asking for your help seemed to be the only way. The last resort, really.'

She took me into the front room and made us a pot of tea and we sat in the bay window.

'It's good to see you, Mrs Patterson.'

'I wish I felt better, David. But ever since the end of term last year, I've felt as if I've been living in a thick fog. My body jangles with nerves all the time. At any sudden noise I jump like I've had an electric shock. I sweat. I become breathless. I can't sleep. I hear a constant high whining sound. And I have never felt like this in my life. My mother used to call it a nervous breakdown.'

'What happened?'

'It came on me suddenly like a curse, after spending some time looking at the work you produced for your final exam.'

'The one that got me a fail?'

'Well, yes. I thought of it as just a formless abstract painting, at least it looks like it at first. A lot of thick black acrylic loaded up onto the canvas. In fact, at the time I was going to tell you off for wasting so much paint. I brought it home with a view to recycling it, to be honest. But the more I stared at it the more I began to think I could see things in the rough brush strokes and palette marks. There appeared to be discernable shapes and recognisable lines – the traces of objects, the outlines of hills, trees, faces. But everything seemed to be always moving and impossible to find again or to explain to anyone else. However, it wasn't so much the real things I thought I could see, it was more the powerful feelings which seemed to be trapped inside the paint. It made me freeze to look at it. I was unable to move away. It felt as though I was unable to even close my eyes when I was standing in front of that square of blackness. I was mesmerised. By your painting, David, by your work. I could sense certain feelings on the canvas being released from the picture's surface and entering my soul like invisible toxic spores that floated into my heart and locked themselves away in there.'

At this point I saw Mr Patterson coming up the drive and he let himself in, put his straw hat down on a chair, and joined us at the table.

'Where is the painting now?' I said.

'How much have you told him?' said Mr Patterson.

'Everything, everything,' she said.

He sighed and sat back abruptly, as if his body had been held in a vice and then suddenly released. The process of asking for help was like the delivery of the help itself, the solution to the couple's grief. Because that's what it felt like; a third entity who had lived with them had died and they had found a possible way to bring it back.

'Good,' he said, very softly. 'Good that it's all out now.'

'It's in the cellar, facing the wall,' Mrs Patterson said to me.

'And how about you, Mr Patterson? Have you looked at it?'

'Yes. But it had no effect on me. It was just – just paint. What did you do, David, when you made this work?'

'I made it the way I make all my pieces. Poured a load of paint on and swirled it around. It was meant to be about a time I was bullied at school, a dark time. A time when I couldn't see a way out. So I tried to make that feeling out of paint.'

Jane showed me her art studio. Canvasses and easels everywhere. Lots of different-sized brushes and tubes of paints. A low table with a kettle, tea and coffee, mugs and biscuits. Shelves full of glossy art books. A nice soft chair to sit in while you think about your work.

I sat down in the nice soft chair.

'You can come here as often as you like,' she said, 'and make whatever work you want. But one thing please; I would like you to show me everything you make and let me spend as much time with it as I need.'

I looked out of the window. The sky was dark and cloudy with a violet tinge to the clouds. I thought about the way paint on a canvas could have an effect on somebody's mind. I never really knew what I was doing, I just threw the paint on and hoped. But maybe I could learn. Maybe I could paint something to change my own way of looking at the world. I wouldn't need to go wild swimming after all. This could be the button that reset my mind, the thing that would release the relaxed and happy person that I knew was hiding somewhere deep down inside me.

The Table

WHEN I WAS born, nobody liked me. I was niche. Pretentious, even. I smelled more of the factory than of the artisanal workshop. More of the masses than the individual. There was something totalitarian about me, and this turned a lot of the older people off. My legs were too thin. My surfaces too smooth. They worried I would not age well. I had a Scandinavian manner that, for some tastes back then, was too informal. I was glued not jointed, and probably made from a template, each part of me rolled in from a remote part of the shop floor, to be assembled, rather than forged as one whole thing.

Now everybody wants me.

The problem is some people want me too much and for the wrong reasons.

◊

I didn't know Olivia that well, she was an acquaintance from my law centre days, but every few years we would catch up and each time we did she would take me to a bar, pull her chair up close to mine and say, 'What's the matter?'

This time she seemed different, more focused on herself. She was no longer working at the law centre and was now a freelance psychotherapist working from her home in the countryside outside Penrith, where she lived with her new husband, Roger. I was then working for the legal services commission, the regulation body for law centres, so I expected our relationship to be a little more strained as I was now a poacher turned gamekeeper, so to speak.

Olivia had changed a lot. Her long black hair had large swathes of grey through it, but in her case, rather than this seeming like a sign of decay, these silver swooshes had the appearance of exuberant flashes of glamour – an advertisement for a wanton pleasure in life. Her clothes spoke the same language; a biker jacket, a pleated nylon-looking two-tone skirt that shimmered between greens and blues, white ankle-height zip-up boots, Chanel sunglasses, and a blue plastic necklace that spelled the word European. It was January 2017, and we were just getting used to the idea of Brexit.

This time she didn't pull her chair up close to mine, didn't lean in towards my face, and didn't ask me what was the matter.

'I have this table,' she said. 'And I desperately need to sell it before the end of next week.'

'What kind of table?'

'G Plan.'

Olivia knew I had a soft spot for 1970s furniture and I was already imagining the dinner gatherings I would have around this cool specimen of mock-Danish design. That right-on couple from the law centre would soon be gushing about my impeccable taste.

'Can you send me the link?'

'Roger says the internet leaves too many trails. We have a card up in Morrisons. Just leave an offer on the answering machine.'

◊

A few weeks later the house phone rang and my wife and I jumped, as only my mother ever rang the landline and she had passed away the year before.

'Congratulations,' said Olivia's voice at the other end.

The table was apparently enormous so on Olivia's advice I had to hire a very particular size of car – a large Renault 4 × 4. I have to admit I enjoyed the drive up the M6, loving the feeling of being high up above the other traffic. However, the pleasure soon dissipated as I hit rain at Forton Services and the sky grew so dark and heavy you could hardly see the abandoned spaceship-shaped tower where the cafe used to be, and I had to pull into the slow lane and crawl along through a soup of grey watery air with the wipers slapping double speed. It was a relief to turn off at junction 39 for Penrith. By then it had stopped raining but the sky was so dark and heavy that even though it was only two in the afternoon it felt like twilight. Everything seemed soft and edgeless as if it was all made of the same grey water as the sky, and the street lights were beginning to glow softly even though it was far too early for them to come on.

To confuse matters, the pick-up address was not Olivia's house; it was on a modern estate on the outskirts of Penrith – a complicated labyrinth of winding crescents and cul-de-sacs of bland semis with barren front gardens and blank-faced garages. Even the way the doors and windows were arranged made them look doleful and lonely.

Olivia came to the door wearing a long back shiny plastic coat and a red beret and when she hugged me I got a rush of her perfume, which smelt somehow darker than her, with layers of wet earth and rotting fruit.

Apart from the huge G Plan dining table, the house was completely empty; oblongs of unfaded paint showed where pictures had once been, and grubby handprints around the light switches indicated someone repeatedly struggling to find them in the dark.

'What happened was this,' she said. 'My husband, Roger, is a bit you know, crazy, and before Christmas I decided I'd had enough and would leave him. So I rented this house and bought a load of furniture for it, ready for us to move in. But when the day came I couldn't go through with it. I thought, yes, he can be an out-of-control psycho, but as long as he takes his drugs, I can probably put up with him till the girls go to uni.'

'Girls?'

'Five-year-old twins'.

'How did he take it when you told him?'

'Roger tends to flare up. So I was going to just do the puff of smoke thing.'

The wind made a sound like someone rolling heavily laden trolleys back and forth across the floor above us.

'So the escape plan is off, the tunnel is sealed, and everything but this gorgeous object is gone,' said Olivia.

It was indeed a lovely example of mid-century design. A giant beige-coloured lozenge shape with beautiful oval wood grain patterns all over it like the rings of Saturn. It looked like the sort of table you see in a Play For Today on BBC 2 which would have bowls of cheese straws on it and green tumblers of Dubonnet. A lady in long, suede boots and a dress made of string would lean against it and cry while she pounded her fist into a bowl of Twiglets. I was at a stage in my life where I wanted to live for ever in an oblique one-room TV drama where nothing conclusive happens.

'Do the legs come off?' I said.

'Sorry. In those days things were made properly,' said Olivia.

'Then I think we are going to struggle.'

And we did.

After getting it on its side and putting its legs through the doors first, we managed to manoeuvre it into the yard. Then we had to upend it and balance it on the fence to get it over into the front garden. But however well we did getting it out of the house, there was no way it would fit into the back of my hire car, and I was about to suggest giving up and hauling the table back into the house, when I saw Olivia putting the door keys into an envelope and posting them through the letterbox.

'So we can't get this thing in the car and now we can't put it back in the house either. Can I have a refund?'

'That would make it my problem,' Olivia said, her legal mind clicking into gear. 'Now it's yours.'

The weather was getting worse. The wind was howling through the alley and the fence panels were shaking with the force.

'Come to mine for some tea,' Olivia said. 'And we'll find someone with a van.'

◊

I watched the woman and the man drive off in their cars and thought about how exposed I was out there in the gusting wind. Then I felt drops of rain pattering on my top. This was the first time I had experienced weather. I had heard it from the inside of many houses, seen it rattling against windows and I always rather enjoyed it, and wished I could be out there immersing myself in it. I felt that rain was probably an important element of my constitution, a large part of the trees I had been made of. But now that I could feel the drops landing on top of me, I knew that it was not going to turn out well unless I was rescued soon. I had a feeling that this lady and me were not a good fit. A woman on the run. And being on the run and owning mid-century furniture don't go together well.

◊

We went down the A595 for a while and then at a junction I wouldn't even have noticed Olivia turned off and I swerved off the road with her. There were no road signs saying where we were heading and the carriageway was only just wide enough for two cars if both vehicles stopped and then crept past each other gingerly. Olivia didn't seem worried about meeting anyone coming the other way because she sped along at breakneck speed and as I had no idea where we were going I had no alternative but to keep up.

All the time I was thinking about my poor G Plan table out there exposed to the elements and I hoped it wouldn't start to rain again.

Then it started to rain again.

Bucket loads. The road began to swim with it as if we were driving the wrong way up a river and at one point I smashed into a deep puddle and it felt like splatting into a wet wall of mud.

After what must have been four miles or so, Olivia slowed down and took another turn-off, this time onto an even narrower road which wasn't even properly surfaced, and we went along that for another few miles until yet another turn-off down a single track of mud and gravel and on this muddy track she suddenly stopped her car in front of me and I nearly ran into the back of her.

Olivia got out of her car and ran back to mine, and I wound down the window.

Rain was running down her face and a big drop had collected on the end of her nose.

'I wanted to warn you,' she said. 'Roger might be in. So remember – *he doesn't know anything about a table or anything about that house.* So don't mention it. Just say that we used to work together at the law centre and I ran into you in the town.'

I sat there for a couple of moments before starting the engine. On the fence someone had hung up a neatly spaced row of dead moles, and the wind turned them to and fro on their hooks as if they were trying to wriggle off.

I wondered how exactly we were supposed to have run into each other and whether Roger would have taken his drugs.

◊

The Table

I was not surprised that they couldn't get me in the car. There is a reason I don't come apart easily. It's because I am well made. I'm not saying I have proper joints like all that old dark brown stuff. But compared to the current contraptions, with their Allen keys and things like that, I am a well put together hunk of wood. I hope somebody comes to save me soon. I can feel myself warping, and if I warp then there is no cure. I will never extend to seat a party of eight again and that would be a tragedy for me. There is nothing better than the exhilarated gasps of a group of people witnessing the magic of my middle section opening up.

◊

'I don't go out any more,' said Roger.

Olivia had settled us down in front of a wood fire with mugs of tea and homemade biscuits, then had gone off to take the twins to their dancing class.

'Oh, right,' I said. 'Why is that?'

'I saw something I shouldn't have.'

'Oh.'

Roger had a big uprush of curly hair and wore oval-shaped sunglasses and cowboy boots. He looked a bit like Ian Hunter from Mott the Hoople.

'Funny you ended up running into each other,' he said.

'Yes. What a coincidence.'

'Everything that could happen does happen.'

'Oh.'

'It's about parallel worlds, isn't it. Imagine your journey here. In one version you got here safely, in another you crashed your car and died, in another version you ran over an old lady in the market place, in another you drove off a bridge into a river, et cet er raaar, et cet er raaar. I am speaking to you now in just one of those realities but all those other realities are going on at the same time. So you just bumped into her, then?'

'Yes, that's right.'

'On the road?'

'No,' I said, 'In the, er, the car park.'

'Four pounds fifty might not be a lot of money to some people.'

'No.'

'But to me it is. To me it's the difference between one thing and something else. I would have to make a choice.'

'OK, yes.'

'Did you have four pounds fifty with you today?'

'I'm not sure.'

'That's the price of parking in Penrith town centre. Four pounds fifty. Look,' he said, and clicked on the television. The familiar colours and design scheme of Ceefax came on, something I had not seen for a long time.

'I didn't know you could still get that.'

'It's the dark TV. Everyone thinks that they turned off the analogue signal. But would they do that? Of course not. They kept it on for defence reasons, kept Ceefax too. MI6 use it, they say. I like this sort of thing. It's warm technology. Everything is so inhuman nowadays. There's something truly alive about Ceefax. Here,' he said, after scrolling down. 'This is a list of all the car parks in the country and the average charges. It's very interesting. Personally, I don't believe in paying for parking. Paying for parking leaves evidence of where you've been and for how long.'

We sat for a time in silence eating our biscuits and drinking our tea.

'It's properly remote here, isn't it?' I said. 'A real sanctuary from modern life.'

'You probably think the countryside is a peaceful place of quiet contemplation. For me it's depressed farmers with shotguns, barns full of rusty farm tools, and bottomless pits of slurry that will swallow you so hard you'll never be seen again. I'm a city boy at heart. I've always had the feeling that the countryside has something against me and that one day it will take its revenge.'

Then he leapt up and picked some binoculars off the window ledge and looked through them. 'There it goes.'

'What's that?'

'The mud has slipped. That road is not going to be clear for a day or two.'

'What about Olivia? How will she get back to the house?'

'She'll go to her mother's. I'll start clearing it with the digger when the rain stops – if it ever does. But we might be stuck here a while. So just me and you, then. What are we going to do to fill the time?'

I looked outside at the rain falling in the dark sky and saw the blinking lights of a helicopter tilting north towards Carlisle hospital.

'You can tell me again about how you ran into Olivia in the car park.'

He bent down to fiddle with the TV controls and carried on speaking, but this time very quietly, as if to the set itself, and although I could see the reflection of his mouth opening and shutting in the thick glass of the screen, I couldn't make out what he was saying.

◊

When the woman returned later I was relieved. But where was the man, my new owner? He had seemed enthusiastic. He seemed to really like me. I had felt that we were going to have a good life together. She enlisted the neighbour to help and I was bundled back into the house and then the lights were turned off and I was left alone again. At least I was drying out. I could hear myself creaking as the excess moisture left me.

A few weeks later the key turned in the door and voices approached. She was with another young man, a different one. Another mid-century enthusiast. He stroked me, he tapped me, he felt my edges. I was overjoyed. Here was an owner who would really look after me. We would have a glittering life together. But outside the house the same thing happened as before. Again she popped the keys through the letterbox, again they couldn't fit me into the car, and again they set off down the road with a promise that a van would come and reunite the buyer with his new pride and joy.

At least this time the sun was shining. She would be back soon, I knew. This was a pattern. Whatever it meant, I didn't know. But I knew for certain that I would soon be inside the house again sitting in the dark and waiting for more young men to arrive. I am difficult to move, you see. That's my problem. You can't just take me apart and put me together again. I am solid. Some things come apart too easily. And each time you break them down and make them again, the end result is less satisfactory than the time before. And finally, after a few too many times, nothing fits any more and you have to abandon the whole structure and find a new one.

The Water

I T WAS EXACTLY ten years after the event when the *Whitehaven News* rang me and asked if I would be willing to pop back to my home town and do a little thought piece for them on the Derrick Bird story. At first I thought the idea of some kind of celebration for the anniversary of such a gruesome event seemed a cold and calculating thing for the press to be thinking about – but to be honest I needed the money and so I said I would go up there and see what I could come up with, qualifying my agreement by saying that whatever I wrote would be a sensitive piece and not exploitative or sensational. The editor agreed.

'We are the Whitehaven news,' he said. 'It's hardly Freddie Starr ate my hamster.'

I was living in Durham in June 2010 when I heard reports of a gunman running amok and randomly shooting people in the Whitehaven and west Cumbria area. I immediately called my mother and father who lived right in the middle of it all, in Cleator Moor, to check they were OK (they were), followed by my sister, who worked in the library on Cleator Moor square. My sister was fine as well. In fact, she hadn't even heard anything about a gunman running amok. (Since the shootings, the libraries play Radio Cumbria all the time in the background just in case something similar happens again.) I then texted and Facebooked my other west Cumbrian friends and thankfully everyone appeared to be safe. But not all west Cumbrians were as lucky as my friends and family. In a shooting spree that went on for hours, gunman Derrick Bird killed twelve people and seriously injured as many more. He covered several miles, from Rowrah where he lived, to Whitehaven and then out to Egremont, Seascale and finally Eskdale where his car hit a bridge and he wandered off and shot himself in the woods.

No one really knows why it happened.

When I got up there, I decided to stay at the Fox and Hounds in Ennerdale, a small village not far from where Derrick Bird lived, and on the first night I chatted to a few locals about the case. A dour sheep farmer, who never smiled and had a drop of mucous perpetually dangling at the end of his long nose, summed it up for me: 'Everyone said at the time that they were surprised that something like this could happen here, in this so-called quiet rural area. But you know what?' He waved his arm towards the window. 'I'm more surprised that it doesn't happen more often.'

West Cumbria is a strange place. From the iron-ore mining settlements of Cleator Moor and the coal pit communities of Whitehaven to the defunct steel town of Workington and the nuclear plant called Sellafield on the coast, it's a mixture of dead industries and industries no one else wants on their doorsteps, all muddled up with mountains, lakes and sheep farms. Copeland, the main local authority area, boasts the highest average earnings in the whole of the north west (including the northern powerhouse hubs of Liverpool and Manchester). However, this is a heavily distorted statistic which goes nowhere near to describing the real experience of many people living in west Cumbria. Because unless you work at one of the relatively high-salaried jobs at Sellafield, there aren't many other paid opportunities. Numbers on welfare benefits are high, including a high proportion of people unable to work owing to mental health issues. The area scores badly in just about all available indicators of deprivation. There isn't much to do either. The local council's investment in arts and culture is very small, and there aren't many restaurants or trendy bars. At the time of the shootings there wasn't even a cinema, and hadn't been for over ten years. (Since then The Gaiety has reopened in Whitehaven, a much welcome development.) There is a small theatre on the hill outside Whitehaven called Rosehill – David Bowie performed there in the 60s, during his days with a touring mime troupe – and there are a few civic halls, but not much happens in them.

The next morning I went to Whitehaven Library and did a little bit more research about what happened on that day. For texture. And I found out that at the time of the shooting, posters outside Whitehaven Civic Hall were advertising The Whitehaven Male Voice Choir's summer concert, The Cowper School of Dancing's annual show with 100 dancers, and The Big O Blue Bayou Roy Orbison Theatre Extravaganza. I was looking for some link that no one had spotted. Was his daughter in the dance troop? Could he have been excluded from the male voice choir for some reason? Or was the link Roy Orbison's lonely yearning voice and those dark glasses they say he wore to disguise a perpetual sadness?

I went from the library to the pub opposite and had a pint, hoping to get some more conversation out of people. After all, we were right next to the taxi rank where several of the shootings had taken place. Looking about the room at the younger men playing fruit machines and the older men on their own in corners with pints that seemed to last for hours, I began to wonder what you did for fun in west Cumbria and what you did for work. If you like hill walking or mountain climbing, it's a great place to live, especially if your thing is over-grazed featureless hills and regimented plantations of fir trees. Most people who live in west Cumbria, though, are not incomers with walking poles, stout boots and a Wainwright guide in a plastic bag around their neck. Most people in west Cumbria are local people whose families have been there for years. Many came over from Ireland to mine iron ore, and hence there is a high number of people with a long Irish Catholic heritage – especially in Cleator Moor and Frizington, the area where Derrick Bird lived. All about you here, thermometer factories and chemical works sit alongside the desolate beauty so loved, and possibly even feared, by the romantics. I myself lived in Cleator Moor until I was about 17 and then in Whitehaven until I was 20. I never had the aptitude for work at Sellafield. I had an interview at the Dent lemonade factory when I left school, but they didn't think I would fit in. They said I was too quiet. I worked at Frizington Co-op for a while and afterwards for a small pottery in Whitehaven, rolling and cutting tails for piggy banks. But I never found a niche in west Cumbria that I fitted into. The gunman, Derrick Bird, worked as a joiner for an undertakers after he left school, but eventually he, like most other stayers-on, was attracted by the higher earnings of Sellafield, until he had to leave the nuclear plant under a bit of a cloud relating to some missing items he was alleged to have taken without permission. Up until the events of June 2010 he was working as a self-employed taxi driver, and people say he had some money problems which seemed to be one of the things that drove him into such despair that he took out a gun and went on the rampage.

I wandered around the town going from cafe to pub and not a single person had a bad word to say about Derrick Bird. He was quiet and polite, they all said. He had children who he saw regularly and an ex-wife. He had a busy social life, drinking in the local pub (but never to excess) and often going on foreign diving holidays with friends. He bought a bottle of milk from the local shop every day and always said, 'Keep the change.' He owned his own small terraced house that enjoyed a stunning view of the Western Fells, a house that many struggling on low incomes in big cities would love to have. His twin brother, the first person he shot and killed, was perceived by him and others to be the more successful sibling. He owned a motor mechanics business and lived in a large detached converted barn just outside Frizington. There was talk that the brother had been given a lump sum from the father of the two men and that Derrick was promised the same sum later. This money never materialised. The thing about living in west Cumbria is you can't be anonymous. Everyone knows all your business and all of your family's business too. So, unlike in a big city, where you could leave a job and start a new one with brand new colleagues who know nothing about your past, here, you can't reinvent yourself. All of your life you might feel that your own successes or failures are continually calibrated against the successes of your peers and your family. A taxi driver who took me back to Ennerdale told me that Derrick wasn't happy at his work, that he didn't get on with the other taxi drivers, one of whom he shot and killed and two of whom he badly injured. He had heard, this taxi driver who knew Derrick quite well, that he'd been jilted by a woman he met in Thailand.

I got a pint at the Fox and Hounds and sat down to look at my notes. There were lots of potential reasons for him going on a shooting spree. Maybe it was one of those reasons, maybe it was all of those reasons, maybe it was none of them. Maybe something we can't even imagine was going on in his head. What we do know is that he had never been violent before and he wasn't the sort of person anyone would expect go on a shooting rampage. Then again, they never are, are they? The other taxi drivers I asked about Derrick all spoke of him highly. Birdy wouldn't hurt anyone. Birdy was a good guy.

I was just about to call it a night when a large dishevelled bloke walked in and nodded hello.

'I hear you've been asking about Birdy?' he said.

'Yes,' I said. 'Do you fancy a drink?'

This man turned out to have been a close friend of Bird's and we chatted for a while about Derrick's life and he told me a few things I didn't know – like that the members of Derrick Bird's diving club had once found the dead body of a murdered woman in a plastic bag at the bottom of

Wasdale. It became a famous case – the lady of the lake, the press had called it.

'The night before the shootings we watched a DVD together,' he said.

'What – the actual night before?'

'Yes. The actual night before.'

'And how did he seem?'

'He seemed perfectly normal. He was often a bit down, but always a nice bloke, you know. Easy going.'

'And this was the night before he got up in the morning and shot his brother dead, then his solicitor, then ten other random people?'

'Yup.'

'What was the film?'

'*On Deadly Ground*. I can't remember much about it, to be honest. I think it had Steven Seagal in it.'

When I got home to Manchester I ordered this film from Amazon and it came the next day and I watched it right through. It is an action thriller with a little slow-motion martial arts thrown in. A bit like *Die Hard* meets *Enter The Dragon*. I remembered that the story of him watching this film the night before he'd killed twelve people had been known at the time, and the press and media had all jumped on the fact that it was a violent film and that this violence must have inspired Derrick Bird to go on his killing spree. But I've watched the film carefully and although it includes a level of brutality you won't find in *Coronation Street*, it's not a film that is principally about random violence. There's a context, and motives. The film is about an evil oil corporation led by a strange, charismatic and unscrupulous CEO, a little like Donald Trump, to be honest. This company want to extend their already giant oil plant into the nearby land of a Native American tribe who live next door. Already I am seeing parallels to Sellafield and its perceived exploitation of local indigenous people in west Cumbria and I am leaning closer to the TV and writing down lines of dialogue. The Steven Seagal character is there to right some wrongs. Wrongs done by powerful people to the powerless. At one point Seagal intervenes when one of the tribesmen is being racially abused in a bar by a redneck oil worker and he beats the redneck up badly. We feel like cheering at this and I couldn't help thinking about Derrick Bird watching this scene and thinking about all the wrongs done to him and how he'd like to put them right in a similar way. The film ends with Seagal blowing up the oil plant and sending the evil creepy CEO into a bath of boiling oil to die. But before he gets to this there is a dreamlike scene in which Seagal meets with a Native American spirit guide. 'What does it take to change the essence of a man?' she asks him.

He doesn't know.

'In you, I have seen a great spirit,' she continues. 'Are you willing to discover the nature of that spirit? I see what man has done to the world. Deep sadness and suffering. I have chosen you to go forth. And you must teach them to fear. You will fight the most difficult battle but you will find your way back. I will see you on the water when the task is done.'

Whatever the reasons for Derrick Bird's shooting rampage – and I am sure there were more than one – I am certain that he wasn't solely inspired by this film. Strangely, the Derrick Bird shootings were soon forgotten by the nation, eclipsed by events the following month in Northumbria involving an on-the-run small time criminal named Raoul Moat.

I opened up my laptop and began to write. But nothing coherent came. It was just a mess of random events that wouldn't coalesce into a single storyline that explained the terrible crimes. In the end, I stopped trying and shut down my computer. I thought about the farmer saying that he was surprised that these things didn't happen more often and began to wonder – isn't he right? Isn't it more surprising that in this unequal society where many have nothing and a few have everything and happiness and misery are so unequally shared out that we don't end up killing each other more often? Isn't that the question we should be asking? I opened up my computer again and began to type, with no idea where the words that were pouring out would lead me, but happy with the sound of my fingers clicking on the keys, the soft roar of traffic from the street outside, and the bottle of beer on the table in front of me.

The Hands

THERE WAS ONCE a man who didn't know what to do with his hands. His hands always felt uncomfortable. If he left them hanging by his side, they were uncomfortable, if he stuffed them into his pockets, they were uncomfortable. If he linked them behind his head they were uncomfortable. Sometimes he would lay them in front of him on the table side by side and wonder what to do. He would look down on his hands as if they were two dead fish. He would make a tent out of his fingers, a praying action almost. He would scrunch the hands together in a ball, sometimes squeezing them so hard it hurt. But his hands were no more comfortable when they were close together than when they were apart.

Sometimes he would burn the backs of his hands with cigarettes. But even when he burned them it didn't help. So he cut them sometimes, with the old bits of coloured glass he'd kept from his toy theatre, the one that his mother had smashed up when she was drunk. But things still didn't improve.

One morning he woke to find one of his hands resting

against his throat, and he thought that his hand had been trying to kill him in his sleep.

He came to believe that his hands had their own minds. That they possessed consciousness, emotions, and were capable of independent action. His hands were machines that had become self-aware, and as is always the case when machines become self-aware, they were conspiring against him.

He had been fine before he moved to the city. People in the countryside are more in tune with their bodies. They work with their bodies, they are manual. Toiling and sweating on farms and in fields and in agricultural commerce.

Put a man in a city and he forgets what his body is for.

He becomes a brain on a stick.

It didn't take long before the hands made themselves known to him.

He was in Tesco looking for a cheap cartridge for his printer when one of his hands tapped him on the shoulder.

He turned his head and looked at it.

He knew that he hadn't made the hand do it, he knew the hand had acted of its own accord.

He looked away, back at the confusing shelves of printer cartridges, all the reference numbers and technical specifications melting into each other, and then he felt the tap on the shoulder again.

When he looked at the hand again he saw that it had formed its thumb and forefinger together to make an aperture that moved like a mouth.

The hole flexed outwards and inwards like the sucking beak of an octopus and then he heard the voice.

It came from the hand, it definitely came from the hand, because as it spoke he could feel the skin around the insides of his thumb and forefinger vibrating as the words went through them and his palm tensing and pulsing like a throat.

It felt difficult, full of effort, like the hand hadn't spoken many times before.

The words it said were these:

'Help me.'

The man looked away from the hand and around the supermarket aisle to see if anyone had noticed that his hand was speaking to him. There was no one else about.

It was midnight. This was a common time for the man to go shopping because he didn't like to bump into anyone he knew in the supermarket and notice what he was buying.

The man looked at the printer cartridges again and tried to concentrate on finding the right version for his appliance.

He didn't want to say anything to the hand. It was his hand. He didn't want to be seen talking to his own hand.

But the hand spoke again. Its voice was male, and deep and rich and oily like a dastardly older lover.

'I need your help,' his hand said. 'I'm not comfortable with you. It's just not working, you and I.'

The man couldn't understand why the hand needed help.

It was he, the man, who was finding it difficult with his hands.

He had always tried his best to make the hand comfortable.

He'd bought gloves in the winter and was careful not to damage it when gardening or doing DIY.

He also washed the hand carefully after using the toilet.

What more did the hand want? the man thought.

The hand could read his thoughts. He didn't need to speak.

'How about not stabbing fags out on me or cutting me with coloured glass from an old toy theatre?'

Oh, thought the man. Yes.

'It wasn't even a theatre,' the hand went on, 'it was a doll's house that you called a theatre.'

I'm sorry, the man thought. Look. Can I just buy a printer cartridge and then we can carry on this discussion in the car?

The hand moved away from the man's shoulder and back to his side.

With his other hand the man selected the correct cartridge, went to the checkout and paid.

In the car park he used the other hand to open the car and when he sat in the car, he rested the speaking hand on the passenger seat.

He felt that now that it was conscious he shouldn't make the hand do work like some mule, or slave, that he should allow the hand to rest.

He sat and looked at the dark empty car park, the rows of shopping trolleys winking in the lamplights, the night workers busy moving large things about near the skips.

He didn't look at the hand; he looked ahead.

How can I help you, he thought. How can I help you, hand? My hand?

The hand raised itself up from the passenger seat and the thumb and forefinger flexed again, and again the man felt his palm pulsing like a throat and his fingers tingling.

'I think you have the wrong hand,' the hand said. 'I can't speak for the other hand, he'll speak for himself. But me, I feel I belong on the body of someone else. There was a time in history when hands would suffer in silence. Hands didn't understand the feeling of not belonging to a particular body. Now, awareness of these issues and the medical solutions to solve them has moved on. There is no reason that someone like me should have to live with this appalling situation.'

The man sat in the dark car and waited to see if the hand had anything else to say.

'I do indeed have other things to say,' the hand said. 'I have a lot to say, I've stored it all up over the years. But I'll say one thing finally. Unless you can come up with a solution then you will always feel uncomfortable with your hands.'

The man wondered if the other hand felt the same.

'Ask it,' said the hand. 'I have no idea what the other hand feels. Just because we are both hands doesn't mean we all know each other and hang out together and have the same tastes and go to the same places and live in one big house. That's the problem with you people, you just see the similarities between us.'

The man looked at the other hand, resting on the steering wheel. He couldn't feel anything different in the hand. But then suddenly it twitched, then twitched again and then began to shake. He gripped the wrist with the speaking hand but it carried on shaking and then it broke free of the other hand and swivelled about to face him. It made its fingers into a beak shape and the beak opened and shut like an indignant swan and the knuckles above the beak shape were like four bulging eyes glaring at the man angrily.

The man had not been frightened by the other hand. But he was frightened of this one. This one, he remembered, was the hand he had found resting on his throat that morning.

'Man,' the hand said.

The man didn't like that the hand called him 'man', and he wondered why the hand didn't know his name.

'Man,' it said. 'Has the other hand been speaking to you?'

This hand had a high voice and a slight accent. When it spoke, whiskers of electricity flicked through the man's bones.

'Has he told you about how he feels he's on the wrong body? He is so self-indulgent.'

Why did this hand feel differently, the man thought.

'Don't assume I can read your thoughts like the other hand. But, as it happens, I can. And I don't know why I feel differently. We're not all the same just because we look similar. I think we've been through this with you before. Remember, Man, that because I'm your right hand, I was the one holding the cigarette, I was the one holding the broken glass from the toy theatre. You made me do that, you made me torture him. That's not a good way to create good feelings between people who have to work together closely. And I,' the hand said, 'I also think we've gone as far as we can with this and now we need to go our separate ways.'

The man could see how this conclusion had been reached but he wondered whether he had to lose both hands or whether he could keep one.

The Hands

The hand read his thoughts again. 'I think you should get rid of us both and we'll sort ourselves out. But the other hand is more circumspective. He thinks the three of us should have some sort of counselling first. I think we're past that stage.'

The man spoke aloud to the hand – to both hands.

'There's one thing I have to say to you both,' he said. 'It's important for me to tell you this. It *was* a theatre. It was sold as a theatre in a second hand shop. I just wanted to make sure you know that before you start repeating weird things to other people.'

'Yes yes,' the hand said. 'But we need to know what you're going to do about the long term.'

Then the hand seemed to suddenly tire of speaking, and it went from a beak to a set of fingers again, and its four glaring eyes turned away from him and it rested itself back on the steering wheel.

The man looked down at the other hand resting on the passenger seat.

That hand didn't say anything else.

The other hand didn't say anything else either.

They sat there, the man and his hands, for hours, until the sky filled with a milky morning light and cars began to appear for pre-work shopping.

At this point the man lifted the left hand and placed it on the gear stick. With the other hand he inserted the ignition key and started the engine.

As he glided through the car park, he looked at the hands and they didn't appear to be about to speak again. He wondered whether they only spoke at night.

This seemed likely.

He wondered whether they would ever speak again. Nevertheless, what they said had been put out there and now he had to act.

That evening he assembled the tools he needed.

A sharp butcher's saw and an axe.

A receptacle for the blood.

Plastic sheets for the floor.

Two bottles of Jack Daniel's to numb the pain.

A CD of thrash metal, the loud noise of which would help to distract him from the task.

He laid all these things out. He and the hands. The hands helped him. So if the hands were helping him, it must be the right thing to do.

The only problem was once he had cut off both hands he would probably bleed to death.

Plus he would not be able to pick them up and take them anywhere.

He took off his shirt and kneeled down on the plastic sheet and placed his wrist on the tree stump he'd brought in from the garden.

His right hand lifted the axe and his left hand rested on the stump.

The man looked at the axe and then at the hand. No one spoke.

Then he put down the axe, and put away the bowls and the tree stump and folded up the plastic sheets.

He went over to a chest of drawers and took out a plastic bag which was tied at the top with a twizzle.

He untied it and spilled the contents out onto the table.

It was a collection of broken glass, coloured broken glass.

The Hands

He picked up a piece in his right hand. His left hand was resting on the table.

He lifted the broken glass up to his eye and looked through it.

Everything looked yellow through this piece of glass. He looked through some of the other pieces.

Blue, red, green, white, purple, orange, all kinds of colours.

He looked up at the ceiling.

In his loft the man had the rest of the toy theatre.

Tomorrow he would bring it down and fit it all back together. He would put the glass back in, he was sure it would all fit.

Then he would use his hands to operate puppets and make up plays which he would film and load onto YouTube. He would do all the voices himself.

The plays would be about psychological problems like feeling uncomfortable in social situations and not knowing how to stand or what to do with your body.

The hands would be happy helping him do this and they would forget their differences.

The man sat down and looked at all the broken pieces of glass and for the first time he felt that his hands weren't there, it was as if his hands were just a natural part of him, an extension of his arms. The hands never spoke again and the man was happy.

The Instructions

MY GIRLFRIEND CLEANED the top of the oven so vigorously that eventually all the instructions were wiped away and you couldn't work out how to turn the rings on and off.

In some ways she was the same; a machine that came with no manual. And because of this, unless she was actually standing there, right in front of me, I found it hard to picture her in my head.

I once noticed that after a night sleeping in our bed, she left no indentation in the fabric.

I sometimes wondered if she really existed.

Maybe she was one of those people who left no trace.

This is a problem for me now that I am in here, because my co-workers often say to me, can you describe her for us? And because she didn't have rusty wire-rimmed spectacles, or dirty red hair, or a mole with hairs growing out of it, or an unusually large nose like a sail, or tiny ears like potato crisps, I struggled to say what she looked like.

'So was her face even and symmetrical, like a quiet day when nothing happens?' they asked.

'Yes,' I said. 'And if you saw her you would say she looked

pretty. But you wouldn't be able to come up with a set of instructions on how to draw her face or how to build it from clay or papier mâché.'

And that is something people often asked me to do in here – can you build her face from papier mâché or clay? Because in this particular workplace we have a lot of time on our hands and a lot of our time is spent describing things outside the workplace – things that happened in the past, people we used to know, things like that. We aren't allowed phones with pictures on them or print-outs of photographs, you see, oh no; the workers in this place can't be trusted with images of people from the outside world.

You might wonder why we have a lot of time on our hands in a place of work. It doesn't seem like a good use of resources; why don't we just have fewer people and get rid of the excess? But that wouldn't work because when we are busy it happens very suddenly and we all have to run to our stations and get down to it. We need every hand on deck. The number of people has been calibrated exactly to meet the demands at the highest periods of customer traffic.

But in the down times, which can last days and weeks and sometimes months – once, a year and a half – there is nothing to do other than talk about the things we remember outside the workplace, the things we might do when we leave, and the things we did when we were out there in the world. And as we aren't allowed images or sound recordings, everything has to be recreated from the materials around us.

One worker has built a model of his town out of cardboard boxes, with small people made out of pipe cleaners, which he moves about the streets and uses to set up various scenes from his life. We all know his town well. We can name the streets and say where certain things had happened to him and even repeat some of the things the pipe cleaner people say.

But as much as I tried to make a model of our flat and the oven with no markings and my girlfriend vigorously cleaning it, I just couldn't seem to bring it to life for the others. And until I was able to do this no one believed that I'd had any kind of past at all.

The Dog

I T WAS A warm Friday evening in the summer of 2017 and we'd just had a late lunch in Mary and Archie's with friends. Everyone had said their goodbyes and gone off on their separate ways, but as usual I wanted to stay out a little longer. I didn't want the day to end. I never did. Because whenever the day ended we had to go home and that meant the day was dead. Being out, being in the world, with groups of people streaming past, with cars and motorbikes roaring by, and with beckoning signs and coloured lights and the whole of life swirling around me, that was everything for me. At home it would be quiet. If we had a clock that ticked, it would be ticking loudly. The house was full of the objects we owned and sometimes the sight of all these things oppressed me. Clare says that we surround ourselves with things that remind us of what we are. Yet sometimes I wonder if these objects represent an image not of what we are, but of what we are desperate to be.

So that night I felt like a night cap, and we walked down Burton Road looking for another bar. Volta and Folk were way too busy, but further up the road we noticed a dark doorway next to the Co-op with a sign above it, white paint on black wood, saying West Didsbury Club.

A plaque said that the club was established in 1898 and other notices told us that Carling lager was £2.95 a pint, a karaoke night was coming up on the 6th of May, and on 19th May there was a reunion party for ex-staff of the former Princess Road transport depot to celebrate the 111 bus route. There was also a photograph of the club's interior, all faded beiges and muted browns, and cardboard signs had been cut out in the shape of stars and stuck on the photo saying that the club had a friendly atmosphere and often featured artistes, the details of which were on a separate board inside.

The door was open and we could see down a brown carpeted hallway, but not into any of the rooms. We stepped inside and got a nose full of that particular aroma that old clubs and pubs have; of heavy carpets infused with beer and antique cigarette smoke, the sweetly rotten smell of tabletops wiped with dirty dishcloths, and the whiff of disinfectant rising out of the toilets.

Music was coming from behind a closed door on our left – *Maneater* by Hall and Oates – and we pushed the door open and entered a windowless room full of velvety red seating and coppery tables. The air tasted of dust and it felt cold, like it had always been cold and always would be cold. It could have been any time of day in any season of the year in any given decade. A couple who were probably aged somewhere in their sixties were sitting at the bar and they looked like they had dressed up to come out; the man was wearing a pale brown suit and shiny black shoes and the woman a bright blue chiffon dress and white high heels.

I wondered if they were on their way somewhere else or had just come back. The barmaid, who looked to be in her fifties, had long brown hair and a creased-up face and was leaning on the bar doing a word search while bobbing her head to the music, which had slipped unnoticed from *Maneater* into *Wherever I Lay My Hat* by Paul Young. It reminded me of the background music you'd have in a charity shop.

'We weren't sure if this place was private,' I said.

The barmaid put down her book and pushed her long brown hair out of her face. There was no one else in the club and the place was massive. Next to the small bar area was a big space with a low stage at one end where I presumed the artistes would be placed and further in the other direction I could see into a large snooker room with three full-sized tables. No one was playing. No one was using any of the numerous fruit machines dotted about the place either.

'It's a closely guarded secret,' said the well-dressed man. 'Have you come about the dog?'

I didn't know what to say and, standing there under the gaze of these three people, I became suddenly aware of how out of place we looked – me with my crumpled linen jacket, brogues and bright patterned Tootal scarf and Clare in her cloche hat and vintage 1960s mac.

'We've always wanted a dog,' Clare said.

'Get them a drink, Marion,' said the man to the barmaid. 'And I'll tell them all about it.'

I ordered a pint of Carling and Clare asked for a dry white wine, which came in a miniature bottle like you get on a train, and we sat down on the bar stools next to him.

'It's a retired greyhound,' he said, 'and the thing about

greyhounds is they don't know how to play. They have no idea how to relax or how to have fun. They just haven't been brought up that way. To be pets, or to be social, to be loved, or to give affection. Have a drink of your beer, it's a good pint in here. Greyhounds have been brought up to run fast and win races and that's all they are supposed to do.'

I took a long drink, maybe a third of the pint.

'Did he win you any money?' I said.

The man paused and looked at his wife as if for advice, and his wife craned her neck over the man's shoulder and said to Clare, 'Come on, love. Sit over here with me.' Clare moved seats to sit with the woman and the woman began right away to talk earnestly to her while gesturing at the walls and the furniture.

'I was never a gambler,' the man went on. 'I picked him up from a feller in here who was moving house. Like I said, these type of dogs, greyhounds, they never learned how to play, and that's maybe why they look sad. Everyone says that, when they see a greyhound. *"Oh, look at* him*, how sad he looks."* So on the first day I took him into the garden and threw a stick. His head followed the stick through the air to where it landed and then he just turned his big sad eyes towards me and stared, as if to say, *why did you do that?* I looked at the stick where it lay and I also began to wonder why I did it. Why does a human being enjoy throwing sticks for dogs? Another Carling? Marion, more drinks for these two. On my tab please. This *not-being-able-to-play* thing didn't put me off him though. It made me like him more. Here is an animal that doesn't have to engage in pointless activities just to fill the time. Like doing crosswords or playing golf,' he looked at his wife, 'or colouring in. The next day we went to the park and I took him off his lead and you know what he did? He just ran round and round in a circle as fast as he could and then collapsed. And he was so exhausted after that run I had to carry him home. The wife, Shirley,' he nodded towards where Shirley was still talking animatedly to Clare, 'she laughed when she saw me carrying him up the drive in my arms, me huffing and puffing while the dog stared up at the clouds.'

The man paused and took a long slurp of his Guinness. Then he said, 'You can't put all that in an advert, can you?'

We decided to walk back to Didsbury Village, as it isn't that far and it was a warm evening and there was no rain.

'That was different,' I said, while we were passing the Co-op.

'What do you mean?' said Clare.

'Because normally in cities no one speaks to you in a pub. It was more like being in the country.'

'Why do you think people speak to you in the country?'

'Country folk are curious about you. They expect to know you. If they don't know you, they expect that they will know your relatives. And if you really are a stranger with no connection to the place at all, they will want to know what your business is there.'

'I prefer to just stare at people and speculate about all that,' said Clare.

We turned off Burton Road and went down Northen Grove past the rusting Citroën DS that was permanently parked there, which we always said we would love to own if we could cope with the mechanical challenges, and then up the little passageway that led to Clyde Road. We crossed Clyde Road and went up Queenston Road, passing the back of the lawn tennis club, and at the corner of Palatine Road, we paused to look at the flattened site of the demolished Peace Inn Hotel – strap-line *live and let live in peace* – its massive wooden sign still standing high on a post, advertising rooms from £30 a night, on the edge of what now looked like a rubbish tip. We crossed Palatine Road and headed up Parkfield Road South where the giant detached houses of Manchester's wealthy stood with their huge gardens full of mature magnolia trees and koi carp. We saw a fox on the corner of Elm Road, and it stood and stared at us before loping off into someone's garden. Then we took a shortcut down Oriel Road which has a nice curve on it as it turns into Oakfield Road, then took a sharp right down Pine Road.

On Pine Road we spotted a group of people in a brightly lit room sitting around a now cleared dinner table, and I wondered if they were enjoying themselves. I mean *really* enjoying themselves.

We stared in at them for a while and I thought about the greyhound. Maybe life is easier if you're not always under pressure to have fun. Maybe that man's greyhound has found true happiness. Why not just run round and round in a circle then collapse? You can lie on the floor and look at the sky. Rain will come in from the west. A million people will go to the doctors. The bulge at the earth's equator will decrease in size. Eventually people will stop throwing sticks for you.

The Process

IT WAS NECESSARY for the process to begin the night before, and everything had to be perfect if it was to have the desired effect. Firstly, I aligned all the objects in the kitchen cupboard. Everything had to be perfectly straight and facing the right way. For a time I was troubled by a non-standard sized coffee tin which wouldn't align with the others, but eventually found a solution by stacking the slightly shorter one behind the others. This wasn't ideal because I knew the mis-sized tin was there, but technically, the cupboard was properly arranged to the casual viewer, so it met the minimum standard. Then I sellotaped the cupboard shut so that Miriam wouldn't open it and move anything out of synch. As it was only for a day or so, I knew she would understand. She always did.

It was becoming more important than ever to have everything right at every stage of the process. The next step was to head over to the local pub and urinate in the middle urinal. Luckily there was no one else in as it only works if I'm the only one there. Then back at home, I found my VHS video of *Kes* and watched it from the 23 minutes mark to the end, then I ejected it and placed it on the top of the fridge, as usual. Miriam would find it misplaced and put it back on the shelf, but that was all part of it. In fact if she didn't do this, nothing would work. I had to keep and maintain an old VHS machine purely for this part of the job.

Then I went to the car and drove out to Chorlton where the McDonald's Drive Thru was. This was the last part of the evening's rituals and had to be carried out with precision exactly as it had been all those times before. But there was a problem; the Drive Thru was closed. A security man in the car park said that there had been a water leak and that it would be open again tomorrow.

I went back to the car and thought. I would have to offset this part with something similar. Offsetting and replacements were possible, and had worked in the past. The time the middle urinal was out of order for example, and I went to the Station Hotel instead, but they had four urinals so no middle one, so I tried the Fletcher Moss which worked fine. And the next day had gone better than expected. So clearly offsetting was a definite possibility.

But offsetting always left me feeling uneasy. Nevertheless it would have to be done and so I set off for the next nearest McDonald's which was in Fallowfield.

I waited in line at the drive-in hatch and when I got there I made my order as usual – a Filet-o-Fish, small fries and a coffee. I turned down the offer to upgrade to a Happy Meal as this had never been done before and would certainly have had the potential to tip the balance in these circumstances when I was already involved in an offsetting procedure.

He repeated my order into the microphone, but pulled a face when the kitchen replied.

'Sorry sir,' he said, 'We are out of Filets. Would you like something else?'

This threw me into a quandary. Should I try a third branch of McDonald's to put the right procedure in place or should I go with a replacement and offset things even further? Bearing in mind there were more procedures to carry out in the morning, and on the way there, so there was always a chance that something else could go awry as well.

I decided to replace it with a veggie burger, as meat would have been just too different to fish, I thought, and went round to the delivery hatch, where it was handed to me after a wait of 7.3 minutes.

Acting as though I had ordered as usual from the Chorlton branch, I drove to the small car park next to the discount sofa store on Barlow Moor Road and ate slowly in the car while listening to 5 Live, which was also part of it. I drank half of the coffee, making a mark on the side to make sure I got the level right, and ate half of the burger, and then half of the fries. The rest I bundled back into the brown bag but I didn't place them in the bin in that car park. I drove towards home and then just after I pulled in at my house, I set off again, found a wheelie bin outside a house on the adjacent street and put the remnants of the meal in there, as I always did. If there wasn't a wheelie bin there, this part could be replaced with another street nearby, this didn't seem to be a major issue and had proved successful in the past.

Then back at home, I ate my dinner without mentioning the McDonald's I'd just eaten and we talked about other things. No words were exchanged about the following day, which is always the way, and the rest of the evening went ahead as usual.

It was an away match at Macclesfield, and, as I lived in Manchester which wasn't too far, I had chosen not to travel on the coach with the others, and was making my own way there. I wore the Stüssy top, Levi jeans and the Puma trainers and also the brown checked trilby hat, which did look a little incongruous, but nevertheless, though I can't remember why, I had been wearing it the first time, and if something works, something works, you don't question it.

The final part was the moustache. I had to find a man with a moustache and ask him if I could run my fingers through it. It had become part of the thing when our ex-goalkeeper, Adam Collin, had a big moustache and for a joke, the team used to feel the moustache to check whether his affectations went as far as using beard oil. When he shaved it off, and this routine was no longer possible, that's when we began to slip down the table again, so I decided to revive this tradition in some part, by finding a stranger and rubbing their moustache. Most people said yes when I told them what it was for. Unless it was an opposing fan of course; that led to all kinds of issues.

In Macclesfield, the agreed pub for away fans was called The Silk Trader so I slipped in there and looked for moustaches. I knew that any Carlisle fan would be happy to help and I found a fan with a big beard and although it had been a moustache without a beard in the past, obviously running the fingers through the moustache part is the same whether the man has a full beard or not, so there was no point being a purist about that aspect. There was a danger you could take things too far if you began to be too strict.

Later, I took my seat in the almost empty stadium and waited for kick-off. I like sitting in empty football stadiums. I like the feeling of space around me as opposed to being in the city where we're all crammed together like dead flies. A nearly empty football stadium was one of the only chances I got to see people who were far away.

The first half was the usually pointless pantomime of hoofing the ball up to the other team's goal, running after it, then falling over a lot. No one scored, until the last five minutes when one of the Carlisle players fell over a bit too hard on one of Macclefield's strikers in our penalty box. The kick was taken and we were one down when we went into half-time.

In the bar I had a Balti pie and a pint of lager as usual, putting half the pie in the bin and pouring half the lager down a drain before going back to my seat.

Nothing happened of note in the entire second half. At one point the Carlisle players were missing passes and falling over so often that our own away fans began to boo them and this didn't help their morale.

At the end of the match I was exhausted. I'm sure I was more worn out than the players themselves, who had no idea what I put myself through every weekend on their behalf – increasingly in vain. This weekend I had put everything into it, nearly two days of hard concentration, and nothing seemed to have worked. I was tired and also a little angry as well, both at the lack of skills and organi-sation in my beloved team and manager, but also with the belligerent Carlisle fans who were keen enough to follow their team to all the away games, yet when the players were struggling and in need of a confidence boost, chose to boo them instead.

I wandered down the road despondently and finally, lacking the energy to get all the way to the railway station in time for the next departure, I went into The Silk Trader where I had found the away fans earlier and sat in a corner on my own with a pint. A man sitting near me also had a Carlisle scarf and was also alone and looking miserable, staring into his pint. It was the fan with the beard whose moustache I had stroked earlier, and when I caught his eye we smiled at each other, shook our heads, and he came over to my table.

We got chatting about our wasted years as Carlisle United fans, following the team to grim towns all over the country, and eventually I told him all about my weekend routines and how effective they had been in the past, but how recently for some reason they seemed to be losing their potency.

He took a long drink then plonked his pint glass down hard on the table.

'I've been doing the same sort of things,' he said. 'All different, but they seemed to work for a while. Maybe we ought to team up. Double the power of the magic.'

I thought about this for a few moments. It seemed like a good idea. Then again, maybe he just wanted me to stroke his moustache a little more, and I leaned over and did so and he didn't ask me to stop.

The Theft

THERE ARE MANY circumstances in which stealing something can be the right thing to do. On this occasion, we were at a party in Scotland when I realised that we hadn't been shown where we would be sleeping that night. A long, cold night on a hard Scottish floor could put us back a long way in the orthopaedic department, so I began to worry. Some people seem to deliberately make it look like hard work to put you up for a night. Whenever I have a guest I try to make it seem as if it everything involved happens magically by itself; the fresh towels, the cellophane-wrapped toothbrush, the code for the wi-fi, the breakfast cereals on the counter, the different types of tea and milk, the conveniently placed key to open the front door in the morning.

But not everyone is like me. There is a certain type of person who, just as you announce you'd like to go to bed, has to drop everything and put a lot of complicated processes in motion to get your sleeping arrangement ready.

In this case, it turned out we were on the blow-up.

'Oh yes, you two. I forgot,' our hostess Anna announced

at three in the morning. 'You're on the blow-up. It's just in the loft.'

So I held the rickety metal ladders while Anna wobbled up them and eventually a blow-up mattress came tumbling down. But on examination we realised that a pump was required. Not to worry, this was in the shed because they use it for the paddling pool. So it was off down the bottom of the dark garden with a Maglite followed by cries from Anna of 'oh no, I forgot that the padlock doesn't work any more', and so on and so on.

'Don't worry,' our hostess said finally. 'I have another plan. You can stay at our friend's house round the corner. We are keeping an eye on it for her while they are in Ibiza.'

'Why are we the last ones to get sorted out'? I whispered to Clare as we followed Anna, who was striding off yards ahead of us.

'I guess we are only outer circle.'

She was right, we were friends of friends. One step removed. Always at the same parties but not a priority. In fact, we had never been alone with Anna and if we ever were, I suspect we might run out of things to say.

Our hostess reached a detached cottage and ushered us inside. A teenaged boy was sitting in the kitchen and Anna called out 'hi' to him but he ignored her and continued to stare at the magazine he was reading which looked to be about survivalism and the outdoors. All around him on the kitchen table were piles of dirty dishes, and these mounds led my eye to the sink which was crammed full of saucepans, crockery and various bit of cutlery. On the floor, wicker baskets overflowed with unwashed clothes. A small terrier was running about yapping, and there were curls of dog shit on the tiles. The place smelled like a hamster cage that hadn't been cleaned out for months.

The teenaged boy put down his magazine and shoved past us to run upstairs and, when he was out of earshot, Anna said, 'That's Harry. He's going to university in a few weeks. But he's having a few issues with, you know,' she flapped her hand around the side of her head to try and describe his mental state. 'His parents are in Ibiza – they thought that a break from them would do him good.' She indicated the state of the kitchen and the dog shit. 'I'm not sure he's coping that well to be honest. I'll have a word with them when they come back. You're in the downstairs bedroom next to the kitchen. Don't forget to come over to ours in the morning for breakfast. Then it's the big bike ride!'

The dog was nice. He was called Stanley and he came into our room and although he did a shit on the bedroom floor, he was friendly and slept on the bed with us all night.

The next morning we took him for a walk by the sea. He tugged at the lead all the time and we talked about how if he was our dog we would train him better. We walked past a library and read the noticeboard, all about the various community activities that were going on in this small town the other side of the bridge to the city. Later we were going on a bike ride. There were thirteen of us and I was amazed that Anna had managed to find a bike for us all. But she had. She had borrowed them from friends and neighbours, and although the bicycles were a mixed bunch, it made me ponder whether it was only in the countryside that you could manage to gather together thirteen bikes from neighbours who would trust you to borrow them. I wasn't sure whether in the city that would happen at all.

'Is it the countryside that makes people more neigh-bourly?' I asked Clare. 'Or is it that the countryside attracts the sort of people who are already like that?'

'Well, the original people in the countryside were just born there I guess,' she said, 'so they must be formed by their environment.'

But I couldn't help wondering whether the nicest parts of the country were places where people had decided to live there rather than being born there. In my experience, people born in the countryside tended to spend their lives resenting the fact that they couldn't take part in any city-related activities and that they couldn't easily get anywhere and that they were perceived as backward. Certainly that's the way I had felt being brought up in west Cumbria. Whereas these kinds of incomers seemed to have shaped the place to become a new sort of town, a kind of utopia I suppose, a utopia built for people who had good jobs and sufficient resources, who could afford to travel to the city to see a play or an exhibition, or could decide just to enjoy the tranquillity and scenery of their rural paradise. Or both. And they chose these towns based on their proximity to airports and railways stations. Towns like Hebden Bridge and Frome and Hastings and Ilkley and Macclesfield.

'What do you think, Stanley?' Stanley had such an intelligent face. The way he peered at us with his head on one side. 'Yes, Stanley, you think the same as us, don't you? And why does that boy never take you out? And why does he let you shit on the floor? It's not your fault. And I bet he shouts at you and kicks you when no one is looking.'

'Are you talking to the dog?'

'Yes. Dogs understand everything from your tone of voice.'

'We could have a dog, you know. Now that we work from home.'

'A Covid dog.'

'Yes, I suppose.'

'Well, let's think about it.'

I let Stanley off his lead and watched as he explored the rock pools and ran about on the sand.

'Don't let him go too far, David.'

'He'll be fine. Watch. He'll come back as soon as we call him. Stanley!' I called. 'Stanley!' But he didn't move. In fact he trotted off along the beach, round the rocks and out of sight.

'I'll go after him.' I said. 'You stay here.'

When we got back to the cottage, Harry was sitting in his usual place with his survivalist magazine.

'Harry, I'm sorry, but we have got some upsetting news,' I said. 'Does Stanley often wander off on his own?'

'I don't know,' he said. 'I never take him out.'

'Well, he's wandered off, I'm afraid. But he knows his way home, doesn't he? Should we just leave the door open?'

'Yes,' he said. 'That will be fine.'

'Do you think you should ring your mother in Ibiza?'

'She said not to bother her with anything.'

'He's a great little dog, isn't he?'

'I don't know,' said Harry. 'He's just a dog.'

'By the way, we aren't going to stay the extra night,' I said. 'We are going to get back to Manchester. Something has turned up.'

'Fine,' he said.

We didn't call in to Anna's to say goodbye. I just sent her a text and mentioned about losing Stanley, saying that Harry was going to keep an eye out for him.

Once we had exited the town, Stanley stood up on the back seat and looked out of the window.

'Do you think he wants it open? You see dogs with their heads sticking out.'

'I don't know. Perhaps he can sense that we are taking him away. Maybe he'll jump out if we open it.'

Clare turned round in the passenger seat and leaned into the back to give him a stroke. 'Good boy, Stanley, good boy. You'll like it in the city. There's lots of parks and lots of other dogs and things for you to look at. It's not boring like in the country where nothing ever happens.'

'What if one of Anna's friends sees him with us?'

'Well, they all look alike don't they?'

'Do you think he's chipped?'

'We'll get him redone if he is. Like how you can get a mobile phone unlocked. There will be the same sort of shops for dogs.'

Green hills rolled past and we saw a large blue sign for the motorway and followed it and when we joined the slip road and picked up speed, Stanley lay down and closed his eyes, as if he knew by the faster motion and the changes in the sounds that we were in for a long session in the car.

'He seems much happier already,' said Clare.

It was true. He looked so peaceful and serene. I switched on the iPod, selected some Brian Eno, and crossed into the fast lane to overtake a removal van. As I passed it I thought of all the boxes inside with the books and furniture and pictures and bathroom paraphernalia and underwear and everything the house-movers owned, packed up inside that one van. That van, I thought, contains the whole of somebody's life, all boxed up and rolling down the motorway. What would it matter if the van crashed and burst into flames and everything was gone? It wouldn't matter at all. For some reason it made me think of the man I once met who liked to buy up garages in his street and keep them completely empty. Maybe you don't need familiar things all around you. Sometime you just need to be loved and everything to be calm and ordered. All your belongings, your familiar things, the things you keep around you that you think define you and keep you sane, maybe they are the things that remind you of your failings. Every day you see a particular thing you bought and think I could have bought something better than that, or how pathetic I was to think that owning that particular object would advertise to the world that I had a clever, creative and sensitive disposition.

I decided that now we had Stanley I would begin to shed my belongings. I would drip feed everything to the local charity shop till in the end our house was an empty shell. And me and Clare and Stanley would just sit there and think about how happy we were.

The Organ Player

B E CAREFUL – you can lose yourself in a city. That was
the warning young people often used to hear, usually
referring to London. I believe it meant that you can lose
yourself morally, and was supposed to discourage teenagers
from running off to the metropolis. But obviously that sort
of rationale acts as active encouragement to most young
people rather than a deterrent. I prefer to think of the
'losing yourself' aspect of a city as more literal. You can
get properly lost if you wander round randomly without a
map. And you can be lost to the world as well. You become
a dot in a pointillist painting of a million other dots. You
can roam around anonymously in the city staring at things
and at people as if you are at a zoo, just taking everything
in. You can't do that in the country. People would notice
you and wonder who you were and what you were doing
there. A city is a real-life computer game, a simulation, an
imitation of life, where anything can happen. In the city it
sometimes seems as if there might be no consequence to
your actions. You can drop litter and no one would tell you
off like they would in a village. You could break something
or steal something. Maybe you could do worse – murder

someone and get away with it. You could disappear, yet live in plain sight of the people you are hiding from. I was always fascinated by these aspects of a city and when things got too much for me sometimes I just wanted to dive into the roar and bustle of a city and hide there as if I was a frog at the bottom of some deep dark pond.

This had been one of those days. I had disappeared into the city for a break from the suburb where I lived and after wandering around for a while had found myself standing at the corner of Newton Street and Piccadilly, looking into the window of the vintage shop which always had interesting ephemera on display.

That was when I saw the dummy.

It was a traditionally styled ventriloquist's doll and as soon as I clapped eyes on it, I heard the ethereal sound of a distant organ playing. I moved closer to the window and squinted in at the doll's inscrutable grinning face and fancied for a few moments that this haunting organ music might be the ghost of his walk-on tune from some working men's club. I leaned in and stared harder at the ventriloquist's dummy to see if anything else might happen. But the doll's plastic eyebrow didn't raise nor did his mouth open up or his ears waggle and I realised that the organ music was not some uncanny paranormal happening; it was coming from somewhere round the corner. The instrument sounded like one of those old-fashioned contraptions they used to have in social clubs in the 1970s – you know the kind: a giant wooden box with a rhythm machine and several keyboards and lots of different settings and big bass pedals. I decided to follow the sound and find out who was playing this music and as I got down towards Piccadilly I saw that it was coming out of a shop near the bus station. A removal van was parked outside and, while the solemn organ music drifted out from the shop's interior, men in hi-vis vests were carrying boxes out of the shop and putting them into the back. The organist was playing *A Whiter Shade of Pale*, its sad, descending bass notes (borrowed from Bach) and the plaintive melody winding around it giving a funereal mood to the slow emptying out of this music store. I moved closer and saw that the shop was nearly completely cleared out of stock and the man playing the organ was stranded in the middle of the room, seemingly oblivious to the fact that he was now alone. I wondered if the men in hi-vis might eventually pick up the organ with him sitting at it and put it in the back of the van and drive off with the music still playing, and him none the wiser.

I wandered into the shop and went over to the organist so I could watch him play – I played the piano myself and had an interest. After a time he must have sensed my presence because he stopped playing and looked at me a little belligerently as if I had been expected and had turned up late. He was a man somewhere in his fifties, but dressed younger, with a hooded top, trainers and one of those atelier jackets with big buttons. He had a well-trimmed goatee beard and on his nose wore round black-rimmed spectacles which made him look a bit French.

One of the removal men lifted two electric guitars off the wall and carried them towards the van.

'Shame we can't support these old-fashioned music shops any more,' I said.

'You can't buy a musical instrument online,' the organist

said, rolling down the cover of the organ. 'It's like a relationship, a marriage even. The instrument has to fit the player, and vice versa.'

He looked around him as if he had forgotten where he was and now seemed surprised that everything around him had gone.

'Is this your shop?'

'I was just passing by. These lot,' he nodded at the men clearing out the stock, 'are high court bailiffs. All this stuff will go up for auction somewhere for next to nothing I expect.'

One of the hi-vis men emptied a cupboard of electrical wires and guitar effect pedals into a bin liner.

'You play professionally?' I said.

'Just a hobby. But who knows what might have been? Sliding doors and all that. If my life had taken a different turn when I was younger maybe I could have been something else. But thirty years in academia and now it's like, well, I just don't fit any more. So I've got nothing else to do at the moment but wander around the town. I'm kind of between jobs. Between homes too. Makes you feel like you're between lives, to be honest. It's sort of liberating having nothing. No one wondering where you are. No boss or wife or friends expecting you anywhere. You feel almost weightless, like you could float away into the sky.'

I looked up at the ceiling and he did too and we both must have imagined him floating up and then hitting the grubby ceiling tiles and strip lights because he laughed and I did too.

'The pubs are open – fancy a drink?' he said.

He looked like a man who needed to talk so I followed

him out of the shop and down a side street to a pub called the Town Hall Tavern.

It was nice. We chatted for a while about music and the Manchester scene and the various unsuccessful bands he'd been in. But just as I was about to go, he said, 'What do you think of Victoria Coren Mitchell?'

'The quiz show woman? I don't know. Why?'

'It was because of her that I ended up like this. I've written it all down here, everything that happened.'

He handed me an exercise book which when I flipped it open was full of tightly packed sentences all written out in a neat hand.

'I'm going to leave it with you. I sense that you might have some sort of connection with the sort of person I am. Read it and then you'll know.'

'Do you have another copy?'

He tapped his forehead. 'It's all in here. Don't worry. Do what you like with it. Maybe one day someone will turn it into something.'

Then he shook my hand and gripped my fingers, holding on to it a little longer than was usual.

'I missed shaking hands during lockdown,' he said. 'I don't know why. Maybe it was just the touch of skin on skin, or maybe it was more. See you around anyway, and I hope you find my story interesting.'

And off he went.

If he told me his name, I never remembered it.

The next day I was heading to Paris for a week's break with my wife and I decided I would take the exercise book with me to look at while we were away. I imagined it would be the self-indulgent ranting of a middle-aged man, or a tale of how life had been awful to him, and maybe some attempts at a Kerouac/Burroughs style of stream of consciousness – as that's the sort of person he looked like. Maybe it would be experimental and drift in and out of poetry and prose. Whatever it was, I felt that it would be interesting. And the fact that it was about Victoria Coren Mitchell also intrigued me.

I got round to reading it on the first day of our holiday while I was sitting on the balcony in the sun and two hours later my mind was reeling from the story I had just absorbed. I had no idea what it meant or what it could teach anyone. I reproduce the organ player's story here in its entirety so that you can make up your own mind.

Whenever somebody asks me why I am so obsessed with Victoria Coren Mitchell, I always answer as fully as I can, listing a few things about her that I think are exceptional, to measure their reaction. The list of attributes varies, depending who is asking. Because it isn't just one thing about Victoria I like, it is many. For example her hair. The fact that it looks a little uncared-for appeals to me more than if it seemed expensively styled. I imagine she washes it no more than once a week and only ever has the ends cut, at a cost of less than ten pounds, in a local hairdressers full of old women. The way she tossed it about to emphasise a point made me think she'd probably had a horse as a child and had liked to comb its mane. But it wasn't just her hair. It was everything. Although she was no doubt very posh, there was a kind of just-below-the-surface loucheness about her that drew me in. Although I knew nothing about her lifestyle, I imagined she liked to drink whisky out of a large tumbler and smoke outside her house under an umbrella in the rain. (I have no evidence of her smoking but I imagine she does and pictured her lips wrinkled tightly around the tip of a Marlboro causing in the future those pucker lines women get from being lifetime smokers.) Also, probably because I was the sort of person who avoided risk whenever I could, I loved the fact that she was a professional poker player, the sort of person who liked everything in her life to be shot through with chance and spontaneity. Danger was nectar for Victoria and I imagined she would enjoy the thrill of speeding along in a low-slung sports car that responded to every bump and curve in the road, excited additionally by the fact that it would probably be Italian and thus likely to break down at any time. And those snooty features. As a working-class lad brought up in the rough end of Bolton, that elegantly contoured pedigree face ought to have been repellent; but it stirred me in some way. I admired her looks, yet feared them too – believing that one day that face could turn to me in anger and with a dry, sad look, hurl me into the outer realms where all the other non-entities dwelt. Indeed, I wondered whether this was something I desired almost as much as I feared. To be belittled by Victoria must have been every schoolboy's dream when she was a teenager; I wondered whether David Mitchell enjoyed being ticked off by this racy, streetwise head girl as much as I anticipated that I might.

There were other things I liked about her. The way on *Only Connect* she manages to build rapport with the contestants, engage the audience at home with interesting facts, while at the same time keeping a tight grip on the format. And all of this achieved in a flamboyant dress and glamorous shoes. Backwards in high heels springs to mind, as the famous Ginger Rogers quote goes. And her jokes: she seems to love not just a joke but the very idea of a joke, relishing the telling and the set-up much more, in some ways, than the actual punchline which, rather than declaiming with a drum-roll, she allowed to leak out with a sigh, leaving us not with a feeling of elation but more one of grief; because now she had completed its telling, the world of the joke had ended and she could no longer live within its wonderful walls.

Her intellect seems to go from nought to a hundred miles an hour in seconds and she had enormous general knowledge which seemed to know no boundaries and ranged across high and low culture. She was as likely to be able to name twelve characters from a Shakespeare play as she was to name twelve hits by Steps.

I didn't always list all of those particular things when someone asked me what I liked about Victoria – in fact there are a fair number more – but I always pick out a few just to see if they shared my appreciation, or could at least understand it.

I thought about Victoria a lot and one day just to amuse myself, I began, as a kind of thought experiment, to examine how developing an actual relationship with her might be made real.

I know that whoever might be reading this will be laughing at me now. No civilian ever gets to develop a relationship with a television celebrity they have become obsessed with. Well, this sort of thing has happened in the past. Not to me, but to others certainly. In fact, it is not that unusual for fans to become the consorts of the people they goggled at from afar.

One day in 1979 a twelve-year-old girl called Gemma O'Neil was watching *Top of the Pops* when a pale-faced androgynous man in a jumpsuit appeared, singing in a high nasal Cockney whine over a soaring electronic riff. She was immediately besotted by this man, who seemed like an alien, a creature who had been sent to earth to save her. The man was called Gary Numan, and as soon as the song was over she took off her shoes and walked into her mother's bedroom and told her mother that when she grew up she was going to marry this man and have his children. Her mother laughed. But nevertheless, she indulged her obsession by buying little Gemma his records and his posters, taking her to concerts, and even round to the dressing room door afterwards to meet him.

And in the end her mother had to stop laughing.

Because when she was old enough, Gary Numan agreed to meet up with superfan Gemma, who was by then the organiser of the Gary Numan fan club, and fell in love with her instantly. She married him and they have been together twenty-three years and now live in California with three daughters.

The only difference between the Gary Numan she lives with now and the one she saw on the television in 1979 is that he now dyes his hair black.

So it was possible, that's my point. It has happened before. So my little thought experiment began to take form. I worked out how my relationship with Victoria would develop right through to its ultimate end. I listed all the steps I would need to take to get to each stage, mapped out the logic flow, and laid out the milestones next to achievable time frames and dates. I also thought about the consequences of this imaginary relationship on my real life, the lives of people around me, and the lives of the people around Victoria. Eventually I had a basic mechanical diagram of how it would work. It was a thorough job. I knew the consequences of all my actions, should I decide to take them. Luckily, I believe it is a good idea to over-think everything. It's only after you have over-thought things that you realise what the consequences of your actions would actually be. If only Dennis Nilsen and Hitler had over-thought some of what they decided to do.

Of course, I wasn't serious about getting to know Victoria. I was happily married to a woman I loved more than anything in the world. I would never do anything to disturb the fabric of my current life. However, my thought experiment ground to an abrupt halt when I hit a particularly tricky barrier.

Victoria's brother, Giles.

Giles Coren.

My planning all fell apart when I reached the point where we would be living together and realised that this would involve socialising with the rest of her family.

I didn't know all her siblings but I was familiar with the screen persona of Giles Coren. And Giles Coren was a character I just knew I would be unable to get along with. I disliked Giles Coren intensely. He was an opinionated, privileged, upper class know-all who seemed to ooze entitlement with every word he spoke. There was nothing about wine and food you could tell him that he didn't already know and know more. All he seemed to be was an expert in being a pointless toff. How could I get along with this upper-class twit from central casting? This privileged Tory-voting twat?

But was I worrying too much? Surely I'd had to deal with difficult unlikeable brothers-in-law in the past?

It was then I realised something that I had never realised in all my life.

I had never dated or married a girl or woman with a brother.

Of the two wives I had so far in my life, my current wife is an only child, and the one before had one sister. The girlfriend I had briefly between the two marriages had one sister and my first long-term live-in girlfriend had one sister as well. I was in the shower when this thought occurred to me and I turned off the water and stood there for a long time thinking about the situation as the unrinsed soap ran down onto my shoulders and the chilly air through the open door made me shiver.

I looked at my watch on the sink.

It was 10.54 in the morning on the 8th September 2020 and I was 59 years old.

Yet it had taken me this long to realise I had never been the boyfriend or partner of a woman with a brother.

How could this be the case? And was it significant?

I began to work out how this pattern could have emerged. Had I sought out women without brothers so I wouldn't have to in some way compete with them? Or be unfavourably compared to them? No. I knew this wasn't the case. I never found out until much later how many siblings a girl had or whether she had a brother or not, and I can't remember any occasions when I had found out that there was a brother and I had then given up on the particular woman. I could only conclude from this that it had been the woman's choice which had influenced this strange set of circumstances. Maybe when a woman first sees a man she thinks 'what would my brother think of him?' And if she didn't think her brother would approve she doesn't take it any further. In fact, maybe she only ever has relationships with men who are exactly like her brother.

But what about the girls who have brothers who are exactly like me? Well, maybe the girls with brothers like me have had enough of people like me.

Another dimension to add was the fact that some men met their girlfriend by being introduced by her brother. The brothers were friends of theirs and they had said *meet my sister* and it had gone from there. So maybe it wasn't just the woman themselves who forced me into the arms of girls without brothers. Maybe the brothers were also part of this devious plot. Had my male friends conspired to keep me away from their sisters? And was there a strange quality control process I had been led through all my life without knowing about it, like a complicated conveyor belt where misshaped biscuits are tapped gently towards a different path through the factory innocently believing that every biscuit went down this route and ended up in the same place?

However, there was this one girl in my year at sixth form. A Stevie Nicks type with long curly hair and a pixie nose. She had given me a black pebble with a painting of her face on it which had been made for her by an artist friend. I used to keep this pebble on my bedside table and

I believe I still have it somewhere now. I always thought of her as the unrequited love of my life. Her name was Jennifer McFadden and one day she asked me round to her house to listen to some poetry she had written. She said it had to be read aloud as mere ink on a page could not do justice to the powerful emotions it contained.

When I got to Jennifer's house I discovered that her family must be very well off because the place was enormous. In the hall at the top of an imposing flight of stairs was a massive multi-keyboard organ with a rhythm machine and bass pedals, and a young man was playing it at a very high volume, the bass throbbing and the high percussion sounds twinkling while his hands pulled out stops, flipped rocker switches, and pushed faders up and down.

'That's my brother Simon,' Jennifer said. 'He can make the sound of any instrument in the world with that machine – a whole orchestra at his fingertips. It can even moo like a cow.'

'Imagine that,' I said. 'Why take yourself down the mosh pit at a Ruts gig when you could be playing *Una Paloma Blanca* with a bossa nova beat.'

We never got to her room and I never heard her poetry. At the end of the year, she went off to some posh university and never seemed to come back in the holidays – or if she did, we must have moved in different social circles.

I hadn't thought about Jennifer McFadden for a long time. But now that I had remembered her, I went upstairs to search for the pebble with her face on it. Everything that was wrong with my life could now be corrected. All that was required was a little bit of research.

◊

And that's how the organ-playing man's story stopped. Right there. In the middle.

Later that evening we went to our favourite bar in Paris, an unassuming café in Butte-aux-Cailles, on a roundabout near an orthopaedic hospital, and we settled down to watch the traffic while we eavesdropped on the people with their limbs in casts who came into the bar after their hospital consultations.

'I've been reading that thing I told you about, from the man who played the organ in the shop,' I said after a while.

'Oh yes – was it interesting?'

'It was all about an obsession that turned out to be the fact that he had never had a girlfriend with a brother. This revelation seems to have affected him badly, destroyed his life, I think. I just can't work out how.'

'Well, I don't have any brothers, do I? And nor did your ex.'

'That's right,' I said, 'and I wonder whether he and I having this in common drew us together in some way?'

'That sounds a bit weird. You know what, darling? I wouldn't think too much about it.'

We sipped our wine and stared ahead. Then we discussed the way French drivers who were already on the roundabout gave way to traffic trying to join – which was completely different to the way we used traffic roundabouts in England.

'So you don't think it's a problem,' I said after a while.

'Giving way to traffic joining the roundabout?'

'No – only ever having girlfriends without brothers.'

'I really don't think it makes any difference.'

When I got back to Manchester, I couldn't stop thinking about that lonely organ player and wondering what he had decided to do about that unrequited love and his never having had a girlfriend with a brother, and how all this had led to his life falling apart. So one day I walked all over town looking for him. Not only did I want to prevent him doing anything stupid but I also wanted to tell him about my own revelation and how it had affected my thinking too. I wondered whether he could teach me something. But he was not to be found in the pub or in any of the music shops and I didn't really know where else he was likely to be. But even if I did find him and heard more about his actions, could I, like him, change my life? Could I act on the information? Unlike the organ player, I had a tremulous fear of allowing myself to be swept along by some hidden current rushing beneath me, or choosing some vertiginous form of freedom that would terrify me every day.

Eventually I found myself in Piccadilly Gardens and went up Newton Street and looked in the vintage shop window.

There was the ventriloquist's dummy staring out at me as before, and just then, though it seems a great coincidence, I heard music again – this time, drums. And again I wondered if it was some magical uncanny effect emanating from the doll; we all think ventriloquist's dummies are haunted artifacts full of the memories of their relationship with some tragic lonely music hall performer who has imbued the dummy with sentience and a will of its own. But, as with the organ, the sound of the drums was real. It was someone rehearsing in the club over the road. I went over and looked up the stairs to where the drumming was coming from, but I didn't go inside. I stood at the bottom listening as the player tried over and over again to perfect a sequence of complicated runs across the tom-toms ending in a flourish on the cymbals. I stayed there a few minutes, hypnotised by this repetitive endeavour, until I remembered I had a Zoom meeting at home so I headed off to the tram stop, the repeated drum fills becoming quieter and quieter in the distance until they disappeared.

The Retreat

I HAD AGREED to teach a course on illustration for a week at a place called the Kilberry Creative Centre, which was somewhere in the middle of nowhere in the west of Scotland. I rarely drive, so the only way to get there was a three-hour train to Glasgow followed by a taxi ride of three and a half hours at the other end. Why do creative people believe you have to travel miles away from civilisation to write a book, or compose music, or paint a picture? And why did you have to go to the countryside, where there is zero stimulation for any artist? Oh, a bird just flew from one tree to the other, write that down. Oh, a cloud just moved in the sky, draw a picture of that. Oh, there's a sheep. Oh, there's another sheep. Hey, it's night-time already, can you believe the day went so fast? It's because nothing happened, that's why it went fast. Nothing happens in the countryside. There's nothing to write about and nothing to see and no inspiration. No dissonance, no conflict, no surprises, no nothing. But I needed the money so I agreed to do it anyway despite my misgivings. Maybe it would change me. Maybe I would return home inspired by the bleak empty landscape. Or maybe the fee of one thousand two hundred and thirty-three pounds (plus travel expenses) would help me to understand the benefits.

The taxi driver was called Gilbert and he was waiting for me outside Glasgow station in a large Škoda. When I got in the back I was surprised by how smart the interior of his car was – all kitted out in pristine cream leather with lovely dark brown buttons and switches. I discovered that this was because Gilbert also did a lot of wedding work for a venue near the creative centre called Crear, and he liked his vehicle to look the part for the guests he had to ferry about.

So up the M8 we went and then north along the side of Loch Lomond, turning round on ourselves at the end of the loch to go back in the direction we had just come, down the side of another long body of water called Loch Fyne. Once we were past Loch Fyne we went along a twisting mountain road between great frowning rocks and empty open fields before hitting a more narrow road where we were hemmed in with trees, which in places arched right over us like a tunnel. It was now getting dark, as it was January, and the weather seemed to worsen as the light disappeared. The rising wind moaned and whistled and the branches of the trees crashed together. Then from the gloom a sign rose up in the headlights saying Kilberry 16, and Gilbert swung the Škoda down onto this road, which turned out to be a single tracker for the entire sixteen miles, with passing places in case we met something coming the other way.

'It's a car killer, this track,' Gilbert said, as we bumped along.

After twenty minutes of this, there was another turning

off the single tracker, on to what was little more than a farmer's lane really, and this took us through thick woods until we entered a clearing and Gilbert stopped the car in a courtyard around which was a collection of renovated barns with tall black windows that gave out no light.

'The Kilberry Creative Centre,' Gilbert announced.

In the gloom the courtyard looked large and several dark ways led from it under great round arches. The walls were topped with broken crenelations that made a jagged line against the moonlit sky.

'It's very remote,' I said. 'Does anyone else live around here?'

'A few cows. And see that big building over there? That's Garlands, the high-security psychiatric care unit. See you next week. I hope it goes well,' and he drove off, his tyres throwing up gravel in his haste to get away.

I stood there in the courtyard for a few moments considering my position. All I had with me was my laptop case and my small rucksack, and standing in that empty courtyard surrounded by those dark buildings, I suddenly felt very small and lonely as if I didn't own anything, and I didn't know anyone, and I didn't have any place to call home. I couldn't see any staff and there was not a sound to be heard but the odd cough and grunt from what I assumed to be cows, which seemed to be a long way off. The place smelled of something like lasagne baking – the unmistakable odour of over-fried garlic, cheap fatty mince, sweet tomato sauce and burnt pasta edges that any ex-student can recognise a mile away. Then I noticed a sign that said *reception* had just been switched on so I walked towards it and in through a heavy door to a waiting area dominated by a massive photocopier. I dinged a bell and waited. All over the walls were black and white photographs of creative-looking people posed in the courtyard and around the grounds. They were probably famous, some of them, but I didn't recognise anyone. I checked my phone and noticed that there was no 3G signal, so I was scouring the walls for a sign with the wi-fi code on it when a voice said, 'I know what you're thinking, David.'

A young woman dressed all in black like a waitress approached with a cardboard folder full of papers.

'You're wondering if there is any internet here. I'm afraid not. We are all here to concentrate on our creativity. The outside world will have to take a back seat.'

'Well, if the back seat is like the one in Gilbert's car, the outside world will be very comfortable.'

'Oh,' she said, taking a small plastic bag from her top pocket, 'that must be the dry humour your comic books are famous for. I'm afraid I don't read graphic novels. I never know which order to look at the pictures, so I leave it to the young ones. I'm Maria. Head of Direction, in the Directional Services Department.'

'I bet you never get lost then.'

'There it is again. Humour is a good way to break the ice, isn't it? Many of our learners use humour as one of their tools. You'll fit in well. In a minute I'll show you to your room. But first of all what we need to do is to take away your phone.'

She held out the small plastic bag to receive my mobile.

I looked at her face to see if she was joking. She had a long thin nose with a high bridge, peculiarly arched nostrils, and a high domed forehead. Her mouth remained fixed in one expression and was a little cruel-looking, with sharp white incisors that protruded over her lips. I could see she was serious.

'It's one of our protocols,' Maria said.

'Oh.'

'For all learners.'

I looked behind me at the heavy door, and then up to a high window on the side of the wall. Rain had begun to lash against it.

'But I'm not a learner. I'm a tutor.'

'We don't like to create a division between the people who come to learn and those who come to teach – we prefer the line to be blurred. We all learn from each other here at Kilberry, so we use the term learners. Every learner is allowed two phone calls each week and you can make these calls at any time – just pop into reception here and fill in the phone call request form and hand it in along with your tokens and then we'll get back to you with a time and location for your call.'

'So there is an internet connection here.'

'Oh yes. We need it to run the business side. We are not like the Amish. We have mod cons. But on the learning side we try to keep things as unpolluted as we can. The modern world, with its radio waves and noise and constant media jabber, is toxic, David. You as an artist know this more than anyone. This is why so many people come here to Kilberry. They come to learn, they come to escape, and they also come to change. As I say, just bring in your tokens and fill in the form and then you can make your permitted phone calls.'

'It's like being arrested.'

'You have indeed been arrested, David. You have been arrested by creativity and charged with being an artist! But seriously, there is a reason that all things are as they are here, and when you begin to see it with our eyes and know it with our knowledge, you will better understand. Come along and I'll show you your room. And I'll tell you a bit more about Kilberry and our funny ways.'

My room was on the top floor of one of the barns and had nothing in it but a bed, a wardrobe and a writing table and chair. There was no mirror. The bathroom was shared with two other rooms on the same floor.

'You mentioned tokens earlier. Are there some tokens in my folder?'

'Yes. You have all the tokens you'll need. We don't use money here. Every transaction is made using our tokens, which are known as Kilberry shillings. You can go anywhere you want in Kilberry except where the doors are locked, where of course you won't want to go anyway. When you've settled in you can make your way down to the canteen where we have put out some food for you. There's no one else here in your section tonight as the rest of your learners will arrive in the morning. Do have a good night's sleep.'

The canteen was a long thin room with a long thin table down the middle and benches on either side. I sat at one end where a steaming bowl of lasagne and some garlic bread had been set out for me, and I wolfed it all down as if I had never been fed. It tasted very homemade and had too much sugar and too much salt in it like it had been made for children who liked to eat only sweets and crisps.

◊

The next day I avoided the students (I was not ready to call them learners yet) as they checked in and I managed to get lunch after everyone had eaten theirs, preferring to meet my class in a more formal way at the first session that afternoon.

There were twelve of them and all rather intense. Nine women and three men, ages ranging from thirty to seventy, I would say. The men as usual were a little on the know-all end of the spectrum while the women focused on whether everyone in the room was feeling comfortable and safe, which of course was important. I noticed that several of them wore floppy tracksuits or dressing gowns and some had slippers on their feet while others went barefoot.

I introduced myself, and then we went around the room and they each said their names and a little about their experience of creative illustration, and I have to say none of them appeared to have any knowledge of drawing or indeed much evidence of any artistic talent at all. But I had taught these sorts of beginners sessions before and I knew that people came on these residential courses for many different reasons – to socialise, for the benefit of their mental health, and sometimes just to get away from family life for a time.

Introductions over, I stood up and wrote on the flipchart the words *perspective* and *scale*.

'Right, grab a pad and pencil and we will do a little drawing exercise.'

A student named Jakub, who in his introduction had said that he had been on a reality TV show in Poland called *Married at First Sight* and was famous over there, shot his hand up.

'David, I have to say, I don't know about everybody else, but I feel more comfortable talking about the feelings that I want to express rather than technical issues.'

'Oh,' I said, and looked around the rest of the group. 'What does everyone else think?'

They seemed to agree with Jakub.

'Perspective is important, you see, for drawing buildings and landscapes.'

Alice, a woman in her thirties with metallic-red hair tied up in a side bunch and a shiny nylon Adidas top, put up her hand. She worked as a content strategist and ran a popular newsletter on Substack, so I expected her to be a little more practical.

She wasn't.

'David,' said Alice, 'I feel that one of the reasons we have come here to Kilberry, which is so far away from everything, is to escape from buildings and landscapes. To remove ourselves from the rules of perspective. The idea that "far away" things are smaller and "things closer to us" are bigger, is a hierarchy that not all of us buy into. I'm not sure if you've read *The Tyranny of the Vertical* by Mathieson, or *Landeaters* by Gareth Stone, or *Line Versus Dot* by The Outcomes Collective. Landscapes have been formed by men and industry and it is only with our creativity we can fight back.'

Vanessa, a woman who looked to be in her sixties and wore orange trousers, a red top and plastic yellow Crocs sandals, chipped in. 'Yes – and some of us might want to work in a more abstract way.'

I put down my marker and looked out of the window. I thought about the twelve sessions I had left to complete with this group and the half-hour tutorials with each of the learners individually and felt fatigue creeping up my limbs like hot water up a radiator. I held the silence in the room as long as I thought possible.

'OK, so let's start by finding out who your favourite illustrators are. Alice, you start.'

That night we had dinner together. It turned out that the learners took turns to cook the food each evening and so the quality varied as to the skills of the chef. Tonight was a rather rudimentary curry which had sultanas in it like one from the 1970s. I sat next to a learner called Ralph who seemed to know a lot about the centre.

'Where are all the other learners?' I asked him. 'The people and tutors from the other courses that are running?'

'They are in separate barns, with their own canteen, bar, shop and living quarters. It's important at Kilberry that there isn't too much cross-pollination. They like to keep things pure.'

He went on to tell me that he had been at the centre for over a year and I found this hard to believe, but he explained that at the end of each course you are offered a discount to do further courses and he had just kept signing up for more. I asked him if his illustration skills had improved much.

'Well,' he said, 'I am getting a much better knowledge of myself and what I want to say and what my voice is and how that might best be expressed. So I expect that I might start to put something down soon. But there's no hurry. Creativity is mainly about waiting, isn't it?'

'I think there's a bit of hard work needed as well if you want to really achieve something.'

He turned his head and looked me square in the face. 'You'll be OK,' he said. 'Just relax,' and he patted my shoulder with his hand, then returned to his curry.

In the bar, I ordered a pint of pale ale which was called Loop Juice and had been brewed by the people in Garlands, the nearby secure psychiatric unit.

'That will be two shillings,' the barman said.

'Shillings? Oh yes. The tokens! I have a few here.' I held two tokens out to him, but he shook his head.

'No, you can't pay with those, I'm afraid. They are *your* tokens. You can only pay with other people's tokens.'

'What do you mean?'

'At the end of each session the learners give you tokens to show how much they appreciated your teaching. How many do you have from your first session?'

'None, I'm afraid.'

'Oh well. I'm sure things will improve tomorrow when you've got to know the other learners better.'

He smiled at me and I tried to read his face to see if he was serious, but the shape of his mouth didn't change.

'Maybe I could swap some of mine with another, er, learner?'

'People don't usually like to swap tokens, David. It kind of undermines the ethos.'

'How do you know my name?'

'We are all part of the creative community here. I'm

also leading a few courses, studying on a few as well, and I help out in the shop too. I'm Trevor.'

'Trevor, have you read *Line Versus Dot* by The Outcomes Collective?'

'Yes, of course.'

'OK. Yes. Well. OK then.'

I sat down in a corner and took out my notebook and pretended to write. In the opposite corner a group of my students – sorry, learners – were drinking and laughing at each other's jokes, which were probably about me. Eventually, one of them, Vanessa of the orange pants and red T-shirt, came over. She put her hand softly on my upper arm and traced circles with her finger on my bicep as she spoke.

'You don't have a drink, David?'

'No,' I said. 'I don't have any tokens.'

'I know,' she said. 'Would you like one of my tokens?'

'Well, I need two for a pint of beer.'

'Two then,' she said.

'But what will I give you for them? It looks as though my first workshop was not a success.'

'You can pay me back later. Once we find our level together there will be lots of ways we can please each other.'

I wasn't sure what she meant but I took the tokens and went back to the bar. Of course, once I had my beer which she had effectively paid for, I was duty bound to sit with her and listen to her life story, which I did for one hour and forty-six minutes. She had been a pub landlady for most of her life and had managed hostelries in every corner of the country. She told me all about the profit margins of hot food, the perils of being a brewery-tied house, and how quizzes and open mike nights were the lifeblood of community pubs.

That night I woke up suddenly at two fifty-six am with the sensation that something had gently shoved me, and I wondered whether there had been a tremor in the earth or a momentary acceleration of the planet's spin. I lay there looking up into the blackness. The silence seemed to be a solid, quivering thing, like a high-tension line close to snapping, or something unutterable about to be spoken. I couldn't get back to sleep so I decided to allow my worries to swarm all over me, the way a bee-keeper does with his insects, encouraging them to entirely envelop him, wearing his dangerous creatures like some sort of protective cara-pace. Maybe it was better to immerse myself in my fears rather than rush away from them in panic. I stayed like that for the next five hours and by the time I was sitting in the workshop room waiting for my learners to appear, my nerves were jangling and I was worn out. I'm not sure the bee-keeper technique would make for a bestselling self-help book.

The learners all turned up at the same time as if they had been holding a pre-meeting about me, and they sat there looking at me with worried expressions on their faces. But I wasn't concerned because for this session I was going to try a new approach. I desperately needed to earn some tokens. The way the week was going I would need more than one pint of Loop Juice a night to get through it.

'Right, in this session we are going to focus on emotions and feelings.'

Everyone in the class visibly relaxed and a couple of them turned and smiled at each other. It appeared that this was the right direction to go in.

'Today I want to explore a time when you've been frightened.'

If they had thought clapping was appropriate I think they would have stood up and given me a round of applause.

'I want you to each take a few minutes and think about a time you have been frightened. Then we will share this with the whole group. While each person is telling us their individual story of fear, I want you to listen in a particular away. It is called shadow listening. Listen to what is being said, but also listen to the shadows that the words and story cast as well. Because these shadows may be more important than the story itself.'

Alice had her hand up. 'That's an excellent prompt, David. I also wondered if as well as shadow listening we should think about silhouette listening? Shadow is when the light falling on an idea causes an impression of it to form on the surface behind – but a silhouette is where the light coming from behind the idea causes the shape of the idea to be exposed and shown as more pronounced than the details. Just a suggestion.'

Everyone nodded and tokens were passed along the line which Alice stuffed into her purse.

After this session I had collected a number of the so-called Kilberry shillings and I went straight to the office to fill in a phone call request form, and then to the shop to see if there was anything else I could buy to make my time at this godforsaken place pass more quickly. As well as snacks and drinks and stationery, the shop stocked dozens of strange gifts – mostly exotic trophies from faraway countries, things like Easter Island heads, African masks, Buddhas, Aboriginal shields, Indian bells, Japanese slippers, and dreamcatchers. I was looking at this haphazard collection of curios, when Trevor from behind the bar appeared and told me that Maria the Head of Direction would like to see me.

Maria's private office was behind the photocopier and I had to sit beside it for ten minutes before she called me in, watching page after page of some long document spilling out. When I was finally called inside, she was sitting at a desk with two other women either side of her like it was a tribunal.

'David, thanks for coming. Please take a seat. These are my colleagues Margaret and Eveline, who are trustees of the organisation and who give up their valuable time for free. Now. We have a question for you.'

'Right.'

'Have you had sex with any of the students?'

I looked at Maria, whose face was as cruel and inscrutable as it always was, and then at Margaret and Eveline, who were staring at me through narrowed eyes.

'No. Of course not.'

'Oh,' she said, and glanced at her colleagues, who raised their eyebrows before scribbling in their notebooks.

'It says on your monitoring form,' Maria went on, 'that you are heterosexual, yes?'

'Yes.'

'And there are several women on the course who are attractive, I would have thought?' She flipped over a few pages on in her notepad and tapped it with her finger. 'Alice, for example. And also maybe Vanessa?'

'Yes, but . . .'

'When we carried out an evidence review of the impact of residential creative courses we found that a repeated common feature of the most successful ones was that tutors had sex with at least one of the students.'

'Well, I'm not surprised that these sort things go on but I'm not sure I approve.'

Maria and the trustees looked at me for a long time and the trustees made more notes.

'Do I get tokens for that too?'

Maria put down her pen and angled it so it was exactly perpendicular to her pad.

'David, please don't render everything in such base trans-actional terms. There are indeed emotional tokens and respect tokens and self-esteem tokens. But they cannot be traded for items in the gift shop or behind the bar. They are priceless and invisible. You need to start earning some of them too.'

I sat back in my chair and threw my legs out in front of me like a petulant child. The trustees were scribbling furiously, enthusiastically giving me their valuable time for free.

'It seems that I am always in the dark about the rules around here, and when I challenge anything, you never listen to my point of view.'

'Always and never live in a house on denial street,' said Maria, and the two trustees nodded firmly in agreement.

'Well, I hear the prices on denial street are going up because it's so popular,' I said, standing up and moving towards the door. 'Maybe I will move to sod-it-all avenue when I get out of here.'

I had put my hand on the doorknob, when Maria said, 'Wait. I wanted to let you know something else while you were here.'

'And what would that be?'

'Your application for a phone call has been successful. You will find your mobile in your pigeon hole. You may make your call from the office here using a temporary internet code which expires in 30 minutes. You see, David, we are not monsters; your well-being is a very high priority for us. Please return the phone to Margaret before you leave.'

On the phone, Clare told me about all the goings-on in our street and the various boring messages flying around on the residents' WhatsApp channel, mostly the chair person Nora Duffy going on about bins being left in the wrong place and the need for volunteers for the alley clean-up day, and for a moment I even found myself missing the mundanity of suburban life in Manchester.

The rest of the week was uneventful. We explored together various different emotions in the workshops and I managed to gather up enough tokens for a few drinks in the bar every evening and another phone call to Clare. A few of the students seemed to even like me. I didn't have sex with any of them, but Vanessa became quite friendly, often sitting right next to me in the sessions and stroking my leg absently with her pen while staring at me. The others didn't say much, so I was very surprised on the last day when just as I was preparing to leave for my taxi they asked me into the common room and made me sit down. Alice then said a few words about how great the course had been and then introduced Jakub the Polish man from *Married At First Sight*, who had written a song for me, which he sang while accompanying himself on a piano accordion. I won't go through the words here, but it was a kind of history of my false starts with the group and then my epiphany when I realised what they really wanted and how much they had enjoyed my teaching in the end.

Then they presented me with a whole pile of gifts, some from the whole group, some from individuals.

It was all a bit overwhelming, to be honest.

There was a large spiky cactus. A box of biscuits. A pineapple. An aerial photograph of Kilberry Creative Centre. Vanessa had knitted me a woollen warmer to fit on my cafetière. There was a set of place mats with a group photograph of all the learners on them. What was most odd was that several of the gifts were personalised to me. For example there was a cruet set with pictures of a cat on it.

'Do you recognise the cat?' Ralph said. 'It's your cat – Katoush. We got the pictures off Facebook.'

Alice gave me an ornamental scimitar about four foot long, which was made of glass and filled with a yellow liquid. She explained that the liquid was an alcoholic digestif a bit like Limoncello. The sword had red, green and purple coloured feathers around the hilt and a plastic bejewelled handle.

'And this is the pièce de résistance, you're going to love this. We clubbed together for this one.'

Ralph tugged a cloth away from an easel to reveal an oil painting of a woman sitting under a sea cliff in a rugged terrain with three wolf hounds at her feet. She was wearing a shawl and staring defiantly into the troubled, stormy water, while waves crashed on the rocks. When I looked closer I realised that the woman was an exact likeness of my wife, Clare.

'Oh,' I said, 'I don't know what to say. That's incredible. How did you make that?'

'We found a photograph of your wife on the internet and we sent it to the artist and this is what he made. Isn't it amazing!'

I stood staring at the bizarre oil painting, the cactus, the place mats, the feline-themed cruet set, the knitted cafetière warmer and the long ornamental glass sword filled with yellow liqueur, then realised that they were expecting for me to say some words. I could also see that Maria and the two trustees had sneaked in at the back to watch the proceedings.

'I'm so moved by this generosity,' I said, 'that I don't really have any words. All I can say is thank you and good luck to all of you with your creativity.'

Everyone clapped and cheered, and when the commotion had died down, I said, 'I'm not really even sure if I will be able to get all this stuff back to Manchester safely on public transport!' All the while I was looking at Maria standing at the back, hoping she would suggest I could leave some of it there.

'David,' said Maria. 'Men have landed on the moon; I'm sure that you can get back to Manchester with a pot plant, a few parcels, and an ornamental sword.'

'And a pineapple and an oil painting,' I added, and everyone laughed.

'You're a lucky man, David,' said Maria.

A car horn sounded in the courtyard and I looked out of the window to see Gilbert standing by his Škoda, waving.

It took a while to load the gifts into the back of the taxi and I could see that Gilbert was a bit worried about his cream leather interior, especially when he saw the cactus. But it all went in and soon I felt the gravel spin under the wheels and I was waving at the learners standing in the courtyard as we made our way up the lane into the single track road out of Kilberry.

The ornamental sword was the most difficult item to control as we bumped up and down on the rutted surfaces, and when Gilbert had to suddenly brake for a car coming the other way, the sword got jammed under the passenger seat and the glass must have cracked because yellow liqueur began seeping out onto the plush brown carpet. I tried to ignore it and keep Gilbert talking, but he slowed down and sniffed the air a couple of times.

Then he stopped. 'What's that smell? Is something leaking?'

He craned his head into the back and looked down at the pooling yellow liquid on the floor.

'I can't carry on with that thing leaking everywhere. I'm picking up a wedding party tomorrow. I'm going to have to take you back.'

I protested, saying I would give him as much money as he needed to get it cleaned, but he refused, and began the complicated business of turning the car round on the single track road.

The sword lay on the desk with an Elastoplast over the cracked glass to prevent the loss of any more yellow liqueur, while Maria, Margaret and Eveline inspected it, shaking their heads.

'And this beautiful object was a gift from a learner?' Maria said.

'Alice,' I said.

'Well, David, I'm sure that Margaret and Eveline will agree with me that we can't allow this incident to pass. It would be an insult to Alice who went to the trouble of acquiring this incredible item for you.'

'Can I just pay for a new one?'

'That's a very good idea. A new one would cost a hundred and fifteen tokens.'

'But I don't have any more tokens. Can I put it on my bank card?'

'I'm afraid that won't be possible. All transactions here have to be made using tokens – the tax office will not allow anything else. A week's extra work with a new group of learners should cover it. Don't worry. Margaret has spoken with your employer and they have agreed it will be beneficial for your personality and behavioural profile to carry out some additional work here, rather than going home.'

'You spoke to my university?'

'Yes. One extra week should do it.'

'And my wife?'

'She is in full agreement also.'

Later that night, after a few pints of Loop Juice, I went a bit mad and decided to try and escape. I crept outside into the courtyard and headed into the woods. It was very cold but the sky was clear with a bright moon so I could easily see where I was going. After a time I ended up at the edge of a deep, dark pool, which I stared into for a while wondering what might be lurking in there. Then I followed its edges and discovered it was a type of moat which surrounded Garlands, the secure psychiatric unit. A small bridge crossed it at one point so I went over it and ended up directly at the base of the high perimeter wall.

I looked up at the huge impenetrable edifice. It had the appearance of a castle. Long curls of toilet roll had been tied to the bars on several of the windows and they were streaming in the wind like ticker tape. If I concentrated hard I could hear faint human cries and a metallic rhythmic tapping. I decided to abandon my escape plan and return to the creative centre, but after crossing the little bridge over the moat I must have gone the wrong way because I ended up walking in circles in the woods, passing the same mound of chopped-up logs several times, before I gave up and found a patch of ferns which I sat down in with a view to sleeping there till it was light. But my body began to shake, it was so cold. A dog began to howl somewhere, a long, agonised wailing, as if from fear. The sound was taken up by another dog, and then another and another, till, borne on the wind which now sighed softly, a wild howling began, which seemed to come from all over the peninsula. I had just stood up to begin searching for the path again when I saw the bobbing light of a torch in the trees and heard a voice call out.

'David! David!'

'I'm over here.'

'It's Trevor from the shop. I was on my nightly patrol and I heard something in the woods.'

As he got closer, I saw something glinting in his hand.

'You have a gun?'

'Yes. For the safety of the learners and staff. It's fully licensed and above board. Come with me. We strongly discourage learners from going out at night on their own into the woods. There are wild pigs and we have also released a few wolves as part of a re-wilding project.'

'Wolves?'

'Just one pack at the moment, but we want to increase the number of high-level apex predators as soon as we can, because it is good for the environment.'

When we got inside, Trevor poured me a whisky. 'Don't worry, you don't need any tokens for this.'

'Thanks for rescuing me,' I said.

'No problem.'

'I was looking at Garlands, the psychiatric unit, while I was out there. How come we never see any staff coming and going?'

'Staff do three-month shifts living on site, then have three months off. Like on an oil rig.'

'Job like that, you may as well be a prisoner yourself.'

'It's true. The jailor and the prisoner are as trapped as each other in some ways. Have another wee dram, you look like a ghost.'

When I began my first session of the extra week, I was surprised to see that most of the same students were still there – including Alice, Vanessa, Ralph and Jakub.

'Great to see you stayed on, David,' said Alice.

'I just can't get enough of it. What would you like to do today?'

'Emotions, please,' said Vanessa. 'You must have a lot of emotions to unpack, David. Why don't you do the exercise with us this time?'

The workshops, the lunches, the dinners, the tutorials, the drinks in the bar, the workshops again, the lunches again, the tutorials again, the dinner, the bar, it all went fast because it was a blurred rush of the same things over and over again, and it seemed like no time until I was back in the common room waiting for my gifts and my song from Jakub. But this time there was no song and no gifts. The learners went back to their rooms and I was left on my own waiting outside for the taxi. I waited and waited and there was no sign of Gilbert and his leather-lined limo. I couldn't ring him because there was no signal and the longer I stood there waiting, the more worried I became. Then Maria appeared with Margaret and Eveline at her flanks and made a hook with her finger for me to follow her.

In the office she sat and flipped through a folder, squinting at the pages of text numbers and graphs and marking some of the entries with a highlighter pen. I tried to interrupt, but she just raised her hand.

'Wait.'

Eventually she closed the folder and leaned forward and put her hands together as if she were praying.

'How do you feel about the number of tokens you've earned this week, David?'

'I think it's OK. Enough to replace the broken sword I hope.'

'Remember when you were first offered this contact and

we asked you whether you had yet achieved level four on your learners development certificate?'

'And I said no because it's a year-long course and I wouldn't have the time to commit to it.'

'Yes. Well, how would you feel if you now had the time?'

'I really just want to get going, Maria. It's been great but I think I've done enough for Kilberry now.'

'Myself and the trustees have been discussing your future with us and we think that now is the right time for you to enrol on the year-long learners development certificate course. We don't feel you have reached your potential here yet.'

I laughed and for the first time I realised what the term *laughed bitterly* meant because I could almost taste the bitterness on my lips as the hollow chuckles tumbled out. 'A whole year? That's ridiculous. I can't just go missing from the real world for a whole year.'

'Don't worry, David. We have sorted everything out. We have spoken with the chair of your residents group and she has agreed that you would really benefit from a personal development opportunity like this.'

'The chair of my residents group – what – you mean the street where I live?'

'Yes, Crossfield Road Residents Association.'

'Nora Duffy? She's just a jumped-up busybody who has taken it on herself to claim that she represents the entire road.'

'She said some interesting things, this Nora Duffy. She was very helpful, informative and knowledgeable about you. She said that lately you had been putting out the wrong bins on the wrong days and also that you hadn't turned up for any of the bi-annual alley clean-up sessions. She also said that there had been an awkward issue regarding a new studio you had built in your garden without permission of the residents group.'

'You don't need permission of the residents group. I had planning permission from the correct department of the council.'

'The residents association is part of the democratic structure of the country. Margaret, can you show Mr Gaffney the visual diagram?'

Margaret lowered a screen with a complicated organogram printed on it. She indicated each level with a pointy stick as Maria spoke.

'Here you have the national government, then the local council, then here the town council, here the parish council, here the local ward committee, and under that the individual residents groups. If you respect the democratic structure of a democratic country then I'm sure you will take Nora Duffy's recommendations seriously because this proposal has been put to the ward committee and then the parish council, the town council and the main council, and I'm sure it will be agreed by all these statutory bodies.'

'And my wife?'

'Your wife has also agreed.'

I sat there staring out of the window. A whole year in this ridiculous hell-hole. And all because that jumped-up nobody Nora Duffy said I had put out the wrong bins. Through the trees I could see a disused chimney covered in ferns and moss, tilting over in what seemed to be an eternal, slow motion swoon. The chimney would eventually collapse completely, falling into the soil and leaf mulch to be digested like a pin in Coca-Cola. I felt like that chimney. After a year here, my real self would disappear. I would be merely a vibration, a transient, transparent thing, born to die a second after, and designed to make no impression on anything in the world, like a single gust of wind.

The year passed and at the end of it I have to admit that I had developed a few more skills on the way. Two phone calls a week with Clare was the only contact I had with people at home and to be honest after a time I didn't miss the outside world that much. A year later, it was the day before I was about to leave when I was summoned to see Maria in the office again.

'I have some news,' she said. 'I have been offered a secondment to another job. In Garlands, the secure psychiatric unit. Three months on—'

'—and three months off. Yes. Trevor told me about the shift pattern.'

I didn't say it would suit her, but she read my thoughts.

'I know, I know,' she said. 'Well, we will see about that, David. In the meantime, Margaret and Eveline have put their heads together and they have come up with a solution to cover my role for the next year.'

Margaret and Maria were easy, they had no idea it was coming. But Eveline was quick and got out into the woods in no time. I heard rustling down near the moat and followed the sound, moving slowly through the ferns so she didn't hear me coming. I had to be quick because Trevor would probably have another gun somewhere and be on his way. I found her over the bridge by the high wall around Garlands, standing there shaking and weeping, murmuring *no, no, no,* quietly to the side as if she were speaking to another version of herself, a version that was not going to die but would escape to tell her story.

I don't know if that other version of Eveline did escape and, if it did, I don't know if anyone ever listened to its story. All I know is I'm still here now, stuck out in the woods, in the middle of nowhere, somewhere in the west of Scotland, a three-hour train journey and a three-and-a-half-hour taxi ride away from civilisation, and still every few years I try to get away and every time I try, my efforts are thwarted. But for the first time in my life I felt free from worry, loosed from the trivial concerns of life. Now I can just focus on the small, lovely parts that make up the machine of a day. Watch how each component works with the others to form a ticking, humming toy, chock-full of nothing but itself, with no meaning and no purpose other than to experience how it feels from second to second to be alive.

Acknowledgements

*T*HE COUNTRY PUB was previously published as a chapbook by Nightjar Press, 'The Garages' as 'Insight' in *We Were Strangers* on Confingo Publishing, 'The Staring Man' in *Best British Short Stories 2016* (Salt), 'The Hands' in *PowWow Litfest magazine*, and 'The Dog' in *Confingo Magazine*. 'The Painting' was commissioned by Victoria Baths Manchester, 'The Table' by the Reflex Festival at Waterside Arts Centre, and 'The Process' by LITUP festival in Macclesfield.

I would like to thank Nicholas Royle for his expert advice and support, Tim Shearer and Janet Penny at Confingo Publishing, Richard Hirst for his editorial work on 'The Garages', Jen and Chris at Salt Publishing, and my brilliant wife Sarah-Clare Conlon, who assisted in many aspects of this work including appearing as a cameo role in several scenes.